Kenny
and the
Highland
Ghost

Books by William MacKellar

Kenny and the Highland Ghost
The Soccer Orphans
The Silent Bells
The Witch of Glen Gowrie
The Ghost of Grannoch Moor
The Kid Who Owned Manhattan Island
The Cat That Never Died
Alfie and Me and the Ghost of Peter Stuyvesant
Secret of the Sacred Stone
A Ghost Around the House
A Dog Like No Other
Two for the Fair
A Very Small Miracle
Wee Joseph

Kenny
and the
Highland
Ghost

William MacKellar

Illustrated by W. T. Mars

DODD, MEAD & COMPANY

New York

1 2 3 4 5 6 7 8 9 10

Library of Congress Cataloging in Publication Data

MacKellar, William.
Kenny and the Highland ghost.

SUMMARY: A 14-year-old boy staying in an ancient
Scottish castle with his family befriends and tries
to help the cowardly ghost who lives there.
[1. Ghost stories. 2. Scotland—Fiction]
I. Mars, Witold T. II. Title.
PZ7.M196ke   [Fic]   79-6630
ISBN 0-396-07811-7

For Rosemary Casey

I have been here before,
But when or how I cannot tell;
I know the grass beyond the door,
The sweet keen smell,
The sighing sound, the lights around the shore.

Dante Gabriel Rossetti

1

To Kenny Spencer, slumped in the back of the little MG, the cluster of round-shouldered hills in the distance seemed like nothing so much as a huddle of gray-shawled witches. In his morose mood, it amused him to think that the mist drifting up in thin tendrils from below was actually the smoke from a cauldron in which some baleful brew was being prepared. A sour grin plucked at his lips as the low-slung sports car flashed along the dike-flanked road. The Scottish Highlands! The eeriness of the scene was getting to him already. And it had been only yesterday that he and his mother left Connecticut to join his father in Scotland.

Yesterday? It seemed unbelievable. Yet come to think of it, everything had been unbelievable lately. It had all happened with explosive suddenness right from the moment a month ago when his father had broken the news. United Groceries Holdings had just acquired a small toffee factory in Scotland and Jim Spencer had been selected to run it.

"It's quite a promotion, Nancy," his father had explained to Kenny's mother that day. "I mean, Homer Budlong, my boss, must have liked the job I've done here in New England with Mrs. Kleinschmidt's Frozen Waffles or he'd never have picked me to run this toffee factory for him."

Kenny had said nothing. He had been too sick inside to trust himself to speak. Not that he wasn't tickled about his father's promotion. His dad was the greatest. And it wasn't that he had anything against Scotland. But to *live* there! For maybe years! And just when he had finally started to go places at Scarborough. New England prep schools can be cliquey affairs, and Scarborough was no exception. Actually, it had been only in the last few months, since making the reserve hockey team, that he had started to make friends. Real friends, that is. And now this! He could forget any chance he might have had of making varsity. Ever.

A chill wind whipping his face, he sighed as the recollection of that scene flooded his mind. He had felt sorry for himself that morning a month ago. All of a sudden he realized he was *still* feeling sorry for himself. He knew his attitude of gloom didn't make sense and was unfair to his family, but there it was. He glowered off into the distance at the huddle of slump-shouldered witches bent over their smoking brew. The words seemed to form by themselves on his lips, almost as though his mind were being short-circuited. "I hope you old hags choke on the stuff!"

Mrs. Spencer turned to stare at her son. "What on earth are you talking about, Kenny? What old hags?"

He felt the blood rush to his face. "Sorry, Mom. Talking to myself, I guess."

She studied him thoughtfully. "But what about the old hags?"

His face felt hotter than before. "I mean, Mom, everything around here is so quiet and, well, spooky-like. All that mist and stuff. All at once I began to think those hills over there were actually a bunch of old witches hunched over a cooking pot." He hesitated, then said lamely, "I guess that doesn't make too much sense."

"On the contrary, Kenny, Scotland is a country

that has produced more than its share of stories about ghosts and witches. There has to be a reason why the supernatural seems so much at home here." She let her eyes drift over the deserted reaches of heather and coarse moor grass. "Perhaps it is the light," she said thoughtfully. "Have you noticed the way it seems to ebb and flow from behind the hills? But not a light like we know in Connecticut. This light is softer, not as sharp as ours. Almost downy—"

"Downy?" cut in Jim Spencer. He darted an alarmed look at his wife. "Are you flipping also? The two of you just got to Scotland and already Kenny is having little conversations with the scenery while you discourse on something called 'downy light.' If there is one thing that light isn't, Nancy Spencer, it's downy!"

"Who am I to argue with the new Director of Fraser's Creamy Toffee?" She threw up her hands in an attitude of mock surrender.

He grinned. "Talking about our little factory, the people at Fraser's are really super." He swerved around a shaggy Highland cow that had meandered onto the deserted road. "Incidentally, Kenny, you'll be interested in this. The Works' Manager is Ian Cameron, and he has a son called

Duggie. Same age as you. Typical Scots youngster, I understand. I told Ian about you."

Kenny dredged up a smile. "That was nice," he returned politely. Not that he gave a hoot about this Duggie kid. *A typical Scots youngster!* Probably went around in a kilt and played the bagpipe in the village band. Kenny stifled a sigh, missing his old gang at Scarborough. He thought it better to change the subject. "Anything else new, Dad?"

"Plenty! Fraser's Toffee is really zooming and we've had to increase production for our second quarter. We're trying to get additional space but it's real tough in a small town like Auchterlony."

"How about just adding to where you are now, Jim?" queried Nancy Spencer.

"Thought of that but it will take at least nine months to get the job done. Skilled construction people are a rarity in these remote parts, and we simply can't wait. So while the work is going on, Homer Budlong has given us approval to acquire an old Scottish castle in the neighborhood. It's called Strathullen and has been empty for years. We'll move our administration people there and that will make more space available at the main plant for our toffee production."

"You've really been busy, Jim," Nancy Spencer

remarked. "And all the time I thought you'd be moping around some heathery glen missing your wife." She pretended a hurt expression.

He chuckled. "You don't mope if you work for Homer M. Budlong. Speaking of him, he'll be over here this week. He'll be bringing the sales and profit forecasts for the next fiscal year. The old boy is quite a planner."

"He's a strange man," Mrs. Spencer said thoughtfully. "His only interests seem to be business and food. He's married, isn't he?"

Jim Spencer pulled round a cyclist with a pack on his back. "Matter of fact, he isn't. Never had time, I guess." He swung the car off the road and brought it to a halt before the entrance to a small, whitewashed inn. "Ian Cameron tells me they serve super steak pies here. Let's give it a try."

It was a cheerful little restaurant with bright Buchanan tartan carpeting and a series of Highland prints on the paneled walls. Mr. Spencer ordered the steak pies and Ayrshire potatoes and, while they waited to be served, continued where he had left off.

"And now for the part that's really going to interest you. As you know, I've been hunting high and low for a house for us. Unfortunately I couldn't find anything that I really liked. So I finally decided that the best bet would be for us to take over a few rooms in Strathullen. We'll be away from the office area, in one of the wings."

Kenny's eyes bugged. "We're gonna be living in a castle?"

"At least for a while. Until we find what we're looking for. Meanwhile I'll be able to fall out of bed and into the office."

"A castle?" repeated Kenny in awe. "Man, wait till the kids back home hear about this!"

His father grunted. "Don't get any ideas, young fellow. We're going to live in a castle because it suits United Groceries Holdings, not us."

"Good old UGH!" exclaimed Mrs. Spencer with feeling as she buttered her potatoes.

Jim Spencer grimaced, repeating the acronym. "Good old UGH is right. They've also arranged to have a woman to help you—the caretaker here. I guess in America we'd call her a housekeeper but actually I understand Mrs. Wheerie is a lot more than that."

"Sounds great, Jim! Fabulous, in fact. I never had a housekeeper in my life, far less a castle, and now I have both!" She sipped her tea. "Must be pretty old?"

"Which? The castle or Mrs. Wheerie? Actually she isn't that old. Kind of grim and solemn.

Dresses in black but nice enough. I understand she can do fantastic things with food, which is probably the reason Homer Budlong arranged to hire her."

"And the castle, Dad?" Kenny burst out. "That's the part that interests me! A genuine castle!"

His father smiled. "A huge affair. Got more rooms than the Waldorf Astoria, although most of them don't have any central heating. I understand that part of it goes back to the fourteenth century. Incidentally, I believe that Mary Queen of Scots spent a night there."

"It sounds fascinating, Jim!" Nancy Spencer cried, her eyes sparkling. "Just imagine! We can tell all the people we don't like that Mary Queen of Scots, no less, slept at our house! That will put *them* in their place!"

Kenny's father paid the bill and they were soon back on the macadam road, threading their way between the bleak hills that seemed to hang directly over them like massive thunderheads. From time to time, as the little sports car burst out from behind a wall of rock, Kenny caught the shimmer of water from a distant loch. There seemed no end to the heather-spangled moors and the soaring heights. No end to the sense of desolation.

"Are we getting near Auchterlony?" Kenny asked some time later.

Jim Spencer darted a quick look at his watch. "We should be there in fifteen minutes. It's just on the other side of that mountain over there. Ben Dearg. A mountain is called a 'ben' over here. That's the Gaelic."

It seemed a lot longer than fifteen minutes before they were past the rough brown hide of Ben Dearg and were spinning along a winding, unpaved road. Immediately ahead Kenny could see an ugly red-brick building, a church steeple, and a huddle of houses with slate roofs. The houses seemed to rise one behind the other and gave the impression of a group of inquisitive old ladies peering over each other's shoulders to see what might be going on.

"Auchterlony," announced Jim Spencer as the car slipped past the drab stone houses and out into the open country.

"Where?" Kenny cried. He swiveled his head violently.

"Those houses back there. We just went through it." The bronzed skin around his father's gray eyes crinkled as he smiled. "You've got to keep your eyes open or you'll miss it. And I'm afraid there's not too much of historic interest in Auchterlony except for the ruins of an old chapel where the ancient Earls of Strathullen are buried. Oh, by the way, that rather unattractive brick building is the Fraser Toffee factory."

"Oh," said Kenny. It was all he could trust himself to say at the moment. He hadn't expected much, but in all his darkest nightmares he had never envisioned anything quite like this. He frowned back at the handful of stores and grim, gray buildings. As far as he could see, not a movie. Not a bowling alley. Nothing! The Earls of Strathullen had certainly picked the right spot for their cemetery! The thoughts that filled Kenny's mind

at that moment were black and bitter. He glowered at the empty countryside, too miserable to talk. He suddenly realized that the car had paused on a wide, graveled terrace.

His father pointed straight ahead. "There it is, folks. Be it ever so humble, there's no place like home."

Kenny followed the direction of his father's outthrust finger. He gasped as his eyes took in the dimensions of the huge pile of native granite that seemed to be rising like an enormous pink cloud in the bright sunlight. Six round towers rode the long roof line, forming bold angles that must surely have made the castle almost impregnable against assault. A number of gunports, loopholes, and chunky turrets yielded additional defensive strength, and a grassy depression under the mullioned and transomed windows told of a moat that once encircled the outer walls. But it was the sheer size of the structure and the lavish, yew-hedged grounds around it that stunned Kenny. He had to gulp twice before finding his voice.

"We're gonna be living here, Dad?" Awe squeezed his voice to a whisper. "Why, it's as big as Grand Central Station!"

"Bigger," corrected his father genially. "And a lot quieter. Anyway, as far as we're concerned, we'll only be taking over a few rooms in the east wing." He swung the MG up the beech-lined terrace and brought it to a halt before a series of curved stone steps. "All out!"

Nancy Spencer stepped out of the car and stared up at the castle, a faraway look in her eyes. "It's almost weird to think that Mary Queen of Scots was once here. That she actually walked through that very door." She shivered, although the day was warm. "You know, Jim, somehow I can almost feel she's still here. That any moment she's going to come down these steps and bid us welcome to Strathullen Castle."

Jim Spencer grinned. "You think maybe she was

the gal who kicked off this Welcome Wagon business?" He winked at Kenny.

Mrs. Spencer made a small moue of exasperation. "The trouble with you, Jim Spencer, you have no romance left in you. All you can think about are profit and loss statements. You have no sense of drama. Right, Kenny?"

But Kenny wasn't listening. He was staring. Staring at where a small white face with dark eyes was regarding him from a narrow window just above the great door of the castle.

The next moment the face had vanished.

✸ 2

Anything wrong, Kenny?" It was his father who asked the question.

"It was a face," whispered Kenny, his voice tight in his throat. "It was up there at that narrow window just over the door. Staring down at us."

Jim Spencer frowned. He glanced up in the direction Kenny had indicated. "No one there now."

"But he was there—"

"Look, Kenny, you must have been mistaken. The people who were clearing up the castle for us finished about two weeks ago. There has been no one here since. No one."

The boy shook his head stubbornly. "But I saw it, Dad. A small, frightened sort of face. The skin

was dry and white like there was no blood in it. And the eyes were sunk deep in the guy's skull like somebody had set them there with a blowtorch."

Mr. Spencer flicked a sidelong glance at his wife. "Either Kenny saw something or his talent for imaginative description is finally improving." He grunted and removed a bunch of keys from his pocket. "Well, we'll soon find out. This way."

No one said any more until Mr. Spencer turned the lock and swung the big door inward. For a reason he couldn't have explained, even to himself, Kenny felt his heartbeat quicken as the three of them passed from the sunlight into a huge hall, partially lost in gloom and shadow. The deeply recessed windows were no doubt the reason for the dimness, and Mr. Spencer pressed a switch that illuminated the hall. "There, that's better. Now we can see what's to be seen."

Kenny let his curious eyes drift over the great room. It must have been a hundred feet high, and a series of banners, frayed and edged in gold, hung limply from the rafters. An enormous marble stairway bisected the hall and on each of the lower steps, as though challenging entry to the rooms above, were figures in gleaming armor, each gripping a pennanted lance. Scattered over the paneled walls were strange monastic carvings, great Lochaber war axes, two-handled Highland broadswords, and iron-knobbed targes scarred in forgotten battles. In striking contrast to the old world decorations were rows of modern steel desks that had been set up in the center of the hall. Telephones had been installed too, and typewriters and calculators. It was a typical office scene, provided you ignored the location and the medieval trappings.

Jim Spencer strode briskly into the hall. "Anybody home?" he called out. Amusement touched the corners of his eyes as he glanced at his son. The echo of his voice washed back eerily from the soaring walls. Almost as though a score of tiny, shocked voices were protesting this invasion of the privacy of Strathullen Castle. Finally the last, hushed, reedy voice faded away. The silence once again hung from the rafters alongside the proud banners of a vanished people.

"Well," Jim Spencer said with a shrug, "no one home, I guess. Not that I expected anyone."

"It was upstairs," said Kenny. "The little face that I saw. At the window just above the door."

His father sighed. "O.K., Kenny. Just to satisfy you. I'll be right back."

He trotted quickly past the silent row of helmeted knights, and in the silence Kenny could hear him on the floor above as he moved from room to room, slamming doors as he went. It seemed a long time before he returned, a look of irritation on his face. "Nothing, Kenny. I hope you're satisfied now."

"It was a little scared face," explained Kenny, "white with deep-sunk eyes—"

"There are no faces up there!" cut in his father. "No little faces, scared faces, or any other kind! Only faces in picture frames. Now stop being so jumpy, Kenny. I know it's your first time in a castle, but don't let your imagination run away with you."

"Sorry," Kenny said meekly.

Jim Spencer grunted, then gestured with his right arm. "Now this is where we'll have our office staff, at least until we get other quarters. Now if you'll both follow me, I'll show you where our rooms are. They're old-fashioned by our standards, but they're bright and comfortable. That's the main thing."

"O.K., Jim, you can be the tour guide." Mrs. Spencer smiled at him. "Lead on, Macduff!"

The rooms that had been set aside for the family were all that Mr. Spencer had said, and more. The more, Kenny had to acknowledge, was the sheer size of them. In his room, he glowered at the huge canopied bed. "Will you look at the size of that? It's gonna be like sleeping smack in the middle of Central Park!"

"Possibly a little safer," observed Mr. Spencer. He led the way along a corridor till they came to a huge room paneled in walnut. It was stacked from floor to ceiling with books. Other volumes were piled high on ornately designed tables or scattered haphazardly on the seats of comfortable armchairs. "And this, I need hardly say, is the library.

Just look at these books, will you? There must be thousands of them."

"And are they old!" exclaimed Mrs. Spencer, who had flipped a few of them open. "Some of them don't have any publication dates."

Her husband shrugged. "That makes sense. They tell me that no one has lived here for a hundred years."

Nancy Spencer nodded, a puzzled expression on her face. "Still, they don't look dusty . . ." Her voice trailed away and she didn't finish the sentence.

"Why should they be dusty?" Mr. Spencer inquired. "I told you the cleaners were just through here."

"Of course, Jim." She hesitated, plainly at a loss to find the words she was seeking. "It's just that—well—I have the queerest feeling that someone was reading them lately. Someone who tossed them on these chairs when he had finished."

"The cleaners," Mr. Spencer said ironically. "I understand the Scots are great readers. They even read on the job."

She rejected the small witticism, her pretty face thoughtful as she examined the leather-bound volume in her hand. "It's not just that, Jim. I mean about the dust. It's something else about these books. If no one has been reading them for over a hundred years, why don't they *look* old? Why aren't the pages dry and stiff from disuse?" She laughed a little nervously. "I suppose none of that makes too much sense."

"It doesn't, Nancy," her husband returned testily. "Look, what's gotten into you two? First you fantasize about Mary Queen of Scots greeting us at the door. Next Kenny starts seeing little white faces. And now you suggest that someone has been breaking in here and reading our books! Nonsense!"

A small smile loosened her mouth. "You're right, Jim. I suppose it was just being in the castle. The stillness and the way the light filters through the stained glass windows and makes queer patterns on the floor. Maybe it was the banners and the old standards that got my imagination going. Anyway, you're right. No one has been here—" She stopped as the sound of front door chimes echoed through the library.

"Who's that?" asked Kenny, turning to his father.

"Probably Mrs. Wheerie, the housekeeper I told you about. By the way, maybe I ought to warn you in advance. Mrs. Wheerie is rather a dour type.

She's been through a lot. I understand she's been widowed four times. I guess that would make anybody dour. Be back in a sec."

Kenny's mother raised a quizzical eyebrow. "I wonder how she went about finding four husbands in a little place like Auchterlony? Forget it. I'm being catty."

A horrible thought suddenly flashed across Kenny's mind. "Hey, you don't think she murdered them, do you, Mom? Why, we could all wake up some morning and find our throats cut!"

"Oh, come, Kenny, don't be ridiculous! Just because she outlived—" Mrs. Spencer stopped as her husband ushered in a gaunt, solemn-looking woman in black. The face of the newcomer was V-shaped, the width at the temples sloping inward to a sharp, no-nonsense chin. Her nostrils were thin and pinched, as were her lips, and her straight black hair was pulled back severely over her bony skull. Yet her face was not without a stern beauty, a regularity of feature she seemed at pains to conceal.

"This is Mrs. Wheerie," said Jim Spencer. "The lady I was telling you about, Nancy. Mrs. Wheerie, this is my wife, and our son, Kenny."

"Hi!" greeted Mrs. Spencer in her friendly way.

She extended her hand. "Nice to meet you, Mrs. Wheerie. I just know we'll all be happy in Strathullen Castle."

Mrs. Wheerie looked confused for a moment, clearly taken aback by Mrs. Spencer's friendly gesture. After a moment's hesitation she withdrew a pale hand from under the black shawl she was wearing and acknowledged the other's greeting. "You're verra young to be the wife o' a manager, I'm thinking. Aye, verra young indeed."

It was the first time Freddie had ever seen his mother at a loss for words. Her face went from coral to pink and from pink to tomato red. "I'm not that young, Mrs. Wheerie," she protested as her husband laughed. "But thanks for the compliment, anyway."

"I was no meaning it as a compliment, mistress," Mrs. Wheerie returned. She turned her dark eyes on Kenny. "And ye are the young one, eh?" Her lips came together in shocked disapproval as she regarded the boy. "Why, the poor lad looks half starved! Well, we'll soon take care o' that." She flung off her shawl and rolled up her sleeves. "I'll put the kettle on. Just give me a minute and I'll have the tea on the table for the three o' ye."

"Er—we ate only a little while ago," Nancy Spencer began, before she caught the frown that was gathering between Mrs. Wheerie's dark eyes. "Well, I could use some tea, now that you mention it," she concluded lamely.

The housekeeper nodded in gloomy approval. "I've no use at all for folks who canna clean their plates. All my husbands were grand eaters. The last one, aye, that would be Angus, had just finished a third helping o' my dumpling when he passed away." She paused and her lips moved, perhaps in prayer. "I aye thought it was very decent o' the Lord to wait until Angus had finished his dumpling before calling him home." She shook her head sorrowfully. "Ah, well. And now if ye will excuse me, I'll get things ready."

Kenny waited until she was gone from the room. "I just hope she doesn't have any leftover dumpling," he whispered fiercely.

"That's enough, Kenny," admonished his father. "Don't treat everything so melodramatically."

Kenny grunted. "After what happened to that Angus character, a guy can't be too careful. Three helpings of dumpling! No wonder the Lord finally called him home. One more helping and he'd have burst right at the table!"

Apparently Mrs. Wheerie had prepared for their coming, for there were homemade potato scones, oatcakes, and apple tarts when they joined her in the dining room. Kenny was relieved to see nothing that looked remotely like dumpling. After a little hesitation he picked up an oatcake and gingerly sank his teeth into one of the corners. He could feel it against his tongue, nutty and gritty, yet incredibly tasty. He took a larger bite, and still a larger until the entire oatcake was gone. He was suddenly aware that Mrs. Wheerie was watching him. There was no expression on the finely boned face. "Another?" she asked. "They're freshly made this morning."

"Please, Mrs. Wheerie," said Kenny. He had two more after that, followed by a potato scone and an apple tart with a crust that seemed to dissolve in his mouth without any assistance from his teeth. In all his life he had never tasted pastries so savory or delicious. By the time he reluctantly pushed back his chair, he was convinced. Mrs. Wheerie was in a class by herself as a cook. No wonder Angus had found it so hard to leave the table!

Apparently Mr. Spencer was no less impressed as he leaned back in his chair, an expression of content on his face. "Now I know why Mr. Budlong hired you, Mrs. Wheerie. He has an instinct about people and food. Your cooking is, well, simply irresistible!"

The tall woman placed a tartan cozy over the teapot. Kenny thought he saw her smile. "It's kind o' ye to mention it, Mr. Spencer. It's what all my husbands used to say. That is, before the Lord called them home."

Nancy Spencer exchanged an uneasy glance with her husband. "You mean, Mrs. Wheerie, they all went home like—like Angus?"

Small lights gleamed deep in the unfathomable eyes. "Ye mean after eating dumpling? No. But they were all fond o' the eating. It just happened that, when their summonses came to join the Great Banquet above, they all had just finished getting up from my table."

"I see," said Jim Spencer a little hastily. He

seemed anxious to change the subject. "By the way, Mrs. Wheerie, has there been anyone in the castle lately? You might think it foolish, but Kenny thought he saw someone when we got here today."

The housekeeper seemed to hesitate before shaking her head. "There's no been anyone here since the last o' the workmen left. That would be two weeks ago."

"And before that?" prodded Jim Spencer.

Her thin lips parted just wide enough to let the words squeeze through. "Empty as a grave."

Nancy Spencer glanced uneasily around her. "But somebody did live here, Mrs. Wheerie? I mean, it hasn't always been—er—empty as a grave?"

Mrs. Wheerie's head inclined slightly. "It will be a hundred years ago since any being—any human being, that is—lived here. Aye, that would have been old Nell Dalhousie. She lived all by herself in the castle. They found her body one morning under the balcony. She must have fallen over the railing." Her voice suddenly went flat, colorless. "Or been pushed."

"Pushed?" Nancy Spencer looked puzzled. "But I thought you said she lived here all by herself?"

"Aye, she did that, mistress, and she was ninety-eight and deaf as a post. The Lord could have called her home forever and she would never have heard Him at all, at all." The creases that bracketed her mouth twitched slightly. "My grandmother used to say that the Lord got tired o' calling her, and never a sign she was even listening. Finally He just lost His patience and gave her a wee shove when she wasn't looking. At least that was the story my grandmother heard. It was all the talk o' Auchterlony at the time."

"So, there hasn't been anyone here since," Mrs. Spencer declared. She turned to her son. "See, Kenny? That takes care of that face you claimed you saw when we arrived. All imagination! Nobody has lived here for a hundred years."

Mrs. Wheerie's angular face reflected a nice balance between indifference and curiosity as she looked at the boy. "Ye saw someone in the castle, young sir? But how could that be?"

Kenny shifted uneasily. He felt uncomfortable under the steady gaze of the dark eyes. "I guess I was mistaken," he mumbled. "It looked like a face. A little scared face. Staring down from one of the windows."

She moved a shoulder. "I'm thinking it was simply a reflection ye saw. Aye, these moldy old windows can trick the eye if a body's no careful."

Kenny said nothing. For a reason he could not

have explained, even to himself, he sensed a certain wariness in Mrs. Wheerie's answer. He had a feeling that in some way she was holding something back, something she did not want known.

"But the windows were just washed," protested Mrs. Spencer. "Not that I think Kenny saw anything." She hesitated, regrouping her thoughts. "I suppose it's these old houses you have over here. The memories of the people who once lived in these rooms. Why, even I had the strangest sensation just a few minutes ago that someone had recently been looking at the books in the library." A quick smile relaxed her mouth. "Crazy, isn't it?"

The housekeeper averted her eyes. "Will that be all, mistress?"

"Yes. And thanks again, Mrs. Wheerie. The tea was marvelous."

Kenny's mind was a veritable beehive of stabbing, piercing thoughts as the austere figure in black silently left the room. Could he be mistaken, or was Mrs. Wheerie being evasive about something? Did she know more about the face at the window than she pretended? And why had she been so quick to attribute it to the condition of the windows, although she must have known they had just been cleaned?

But of all the thoughts threshing in Kenny's

mind, there was one that kept returning again and again and again.

Mrs. Wheerie had said that no one had lived in the castle for a hundred years. Then she had added, almost as an afterthought, "Any human being, that is."

Had there been anything behind those cryptic words?

And if so, what?

⚛ 3

It was some time later that the stillness of Strathullen Castle was shattered once again by the
sound of the door chimes. Mr. Spencer tossed
aside the financial report he had been reading in
the library and got up from his chair. "I'll answer
it. Mrs. Wheerie's off in the kitchen somewhere.
Anyway, if I'm not mistaken, it should be Duggie."

"Duggie who?" inquired Kenny blankly.

"Duggie Cameron. The youngster I told you
about. His father told me he'd be dropping over to
see you." He smiled. "I guess he's anxious to meet
a real American boy."

Kenny nodded glumly. *I'll bet.* A sigh of resigna-
tion escaped his lips. Might as well make the best

of it. No doubt the kid had an accent you could cut with a rusty claymore. Might even turn up with his kilt and bagpipes, just to impress the visitor from overseas. Kenny sighed again. Why couldn't people just act natural and stop going around trying to impress everybody? He was still brooding over that thought when he suddenly realized his father had returned.

"Kenny, I want you to meet Duggie Cameron, the boy I mentioned to you. Duggie, this is my son, Kenny."

The American stared wide eyed at the boy trailing behind Mr. Spencer. He was about fourteen, with a shock of unruly red hair that spilled over his ears and down his neck. His eyes were an intense blue and his face was lean, with the characteristic high cheekbones of the Celt. He was dressed in Levis, scuffed cowboy boots, and a black leather jacket right out of "Happy Days." The newcomer relocated the wad of gum he was chewing and extended a friendly hand. "Hi, Kenny. Nice knowin' ya."

Kenny gulped as he shook hands. If his father had just introduced him to the latest manager of the New York Yankees he couldn't have been more dumbfounded. The gum-chewing kid in front of him was as far removed from his mental image of a typical Scots youngster as was humanly possible. "Hi," Kenny finally managed. He tried desperately to think of something to say. "Tea?"

"Tea?" Duggie Cameron's freckles realigned themselves as he screwed up his face in alarm. "Kenny, you gotta be kidding! It's nice of you to offer it but that brew is strictly for old ladies in rocking chairs. Can you imagine those macho merchants in 'Hawaii Five-O' swilling that stuff? Thanks anyway. I will take a Coke, though, if you've got one handy."

"Coke? I'll check it out. Be right back, Duggie." He had only taken a few steps toward the kitchen when he was surprised to see the door swing open. It was Mrs. Wheerie, expressionless as ever, a familiar bottle and a glass on a silver tray. Clearly she must have been listening at the door. She poured the drink, then extended the tray to the visitor. She said nothing.

"Er—thanks," said Duggie. For once he seemed at a loss for words. His eyes followed her thoughtfully as she silently glided from the room like a long black shadow. It was not until the door swung closed behind her that he spoke. His voice was a conspiratorial whisper. "You've heard she buried four husbands?"

Kenny nodded. "The last one was a guy named

Angus. Right after the third helping of dumpling."

Duggie's eyes narrowed. "Four of them! They never had a chance, poor devils. Everyone says they couldn't resist her cooking." He flicked a sidelong glance toward the kitchen. "You know she's a super cook?"

Kenny nodded. "Dad says he's never seen anyone like her."

"I'll bet. And neither had Homer Budlong when he hired her. I just hope the dude knew what he was doing."

Kenny looked at him quickly. "What do you mean?"

"Oh, nothing, I suppose. Thinking out loud, I guess. Like they do in those private-eye shows. Four husbands. All dead from something they ate. Columbo might have called it 'The Case of the Four Stuffed Turkeys.'" He suddenly grinned. "Columbo! Sharp little cookie. No flies on that character."

Kenny stared suspiciously at the young Scot. "Where did you learn to talk like that? Like you were some kind of far-out deejay. I figured from everything Dad told me that you'd be going around saying things like 'Hoot, mon, it's a braw, bricht, moonlicht nicht.'"

Duggie chuckled and took a swig of his Coke. "Kinda took you by surprise, Kenny, boy? The fact is there's nothing to do around Auchterlony except watch the telly and read Whodunits. On the tube I go for the cop shows and mysteries. I don't mean to hype myself but I can usually spot the bad guy before Kojak gets to his second lollipop."

Kenny looked properly impressed. "You can?"

"It's just a matter of training your deductive powers," said Duggie airily. "Sherlock Holmes could do it too. The old boy could look at some guy and tell you everything about him except his Social Security number." He shrugged indifferently. "It's no trick if you know how. For instance, I can tell that you were fourteen on the twentieth of February. That your blood type is O and that you go to a prep school in Connecticut called Scarborough." He rubbed his jaw, his face thoughtful. "Oh, yes, the zip code is 06107."

Kenny felt his jaw drop. "You can tell all that by just looking at my face?"

Duggie grinned. "Not by looking at your face, Kenny. By looking at your father's personnel records! O.K., I shouldn't have, but they came into the office yesterday and I just sneaked a peek. Don't tell my father or he would flay me alive."

Kenny smiled. "I won't say a word. I mean,

you're the only friend I have in Auchterlony, and I don't want you winding up as a crazy kind of rug over the fireplace. Another Coke?"

"No thanks. And sorry for trying to be so cute a moment ago." Duggie let his eyes drift around the richly paneled room. "Some pad you've got here, Kenny," he said approvingly. "Kinda drab, though. I've got a couple of 'Charlie's Angels' posters you can have. Give a little tone to the old joint."

"Thanks." Kenny glanced doubtfully up at the richly ornamented ceiling and the delicately scrolled plaster overmantel above the arched fireplace. "You don't think Mary Queen of Scots would mind?"

"Uh? Hey, I forgot about the old gal! Mind? Not her. She liked music and good times. I guess maybe that was one of the reasons some people didn't like her."

Kenny nodded. "Did she really spend a night here? Dad claims she did."

Duggie shrugged. "No one knows for certain but we're pretty sure she did. That was right after her escape from Lochleven Castle. Her flight route had to take her past Auchterlony. Strathullen is the only grand house of any repute in the area."

45

"Forgive me for being stupid about your Scottish history, Duggie, but why was the queen escaping? I'm curious."

"You really want to know?" The redheaded boy shrugged. "I won't bore you with all the details, but the first thing you have to understand is that Mary Queen of Scots and Elizabeth of England were cousins. If anything happened to Elizabeth, Mary would have been queen of both countries. Looked at in another way, as long as Mary was around, Elizabeth felt there was a contract out on her life. So good Queen Bess beat her cousin to the punch by having Mary imprisoned and later beheaded."

Kenny grimaced. "Things were tough in those days."

"They're still tough. Have you been reading the papers lately?" Duggie laughed sourly. "By the way, this is the first time I've been inside the castle. How about showing one of the peasants how the other half lives?"

"Sure thing," said Kenny with alacrity. The more he saw of Duggie Cameron, the more he liked him. Duggie had an open friendly face that belied his air of super cool. The thought suddenly came to Kenny that life around Auchterlony might not be as dull as he had feared!

46

"My first real look at the place too, Duggie," he said as he led the way into the great hall. "If you don't mind one peasant leading another, I'll give you the two dollar tour. Or maybe you call it the two pound tour over here."

Duggie smiled but did not answer. Clearly he was enjoying himself. His blue eyes, quick and shrewd, seemed to miss nothing as he followed Kenny. It was the redheaded boy who spotted the diminutive figure of a helmeted knight in black armor.

"Hey, Kenny," he called out with professional interest, "this is odd. Take a look at this dude, will you? Then check him out against the others. He must be half the size of the rest of them."

Kenny studied the row of vizored knights ranged along each side of the great central stairway. Duggie was right. They were all of similar height, all except this one figure which barely reached to the shoulders of the others.

"Maybe a kid," he hazarded before peering at the inscription on a bronze plate. The lettering was almost obliterated and he read it aloud with difficulty: "Duncan MacDhu, Earl of Strathullen, 1520–1568."

Kenny frowned. "That would make him forty-eight when he died. So no kid."

"Only we don't know how old he was when he got himself the tin suit," mused Duggie. "He could still have been a kid, but I doubt it. No, I think that this is as big as he ever got." His face split in a broad grin. "Whoever he was, he was living at the wrong time. Can you imagine all the movies he could have gotten into for half price?" He laughed and was about to turn away when some thought seemed to arrest him. "Fifteen sixty-eight! Hey, that was the year the queen was here! We had it in school last year. One of the few dates I remember outside my birthday."

"So the little guy was running the joint when the queen showed up?" Kenny was silent for a long moment, then shrugged. "Oh, well, history, mystery. They're all dead now and pushing up heather, or whatever they push up in Scotland. Let's go, Duggie."

Together they made their way between the rows of armored knights and up the great circular stairway. They walked quietly, saying little at first, curious, more than just a little awed by the grandeur and solemnity of the world around them. For his part, Kenny had to admit he had never seen such ornate bedchambers, such endless corridors, and richly friezed galleries. There seemed no end to Strathullen Castle. No end to the number of recessed arches and scrolled gables.

After a full hour of climbing stairs and wandering along gloomy corridors, Kenny was more than ready to call it quits. After all, how much history could a fellow digest in one afternoon? They had just left a blue tapestried bedchamber with its inevitable series of grim family portraits when something made him pause. What was it? He hesitated, uncertain why he had stopped, waiting for the thought to catch up with the instinct that had brought him to a halt. He looked doubtfully back at the room they had just left. There had been something just now. . . .

Kenny frowned and retraced his steps. His eyes flitted around the room. A delicately wrought longcase clock. A lyre-backed chair next to the blue-canopied bed. An oval giltwood mirror. A portrait. . . . Yes, that was it. There was something vaguely familiar about the painting. Something that had disturbed him without his knowing why. He crossed the room and gazed intently at the oil painting hanging over the mantelpiece. It was a portrait of a small man in Highland costume. The face was pale and timid and the deep-set eyes seemed to be hiding from the world.

"Anything wrong, Kenny?" Duggie inquired as he reentered the room. His eyes followed the other's gaze, and he stared at the portrait before removing his handkerchief and running it over the gilt edging. Then he folded his handkerchief neatly and pulled out a glass, placing it in one eye and squinting at the barely discernible lettering.

"Duncan MacDhu, Seventh Earl of Strathullen," he read. He emitted a soft whistle. "Hey, that's funny. That was the name of the little guy we were just talking about. The little guy who was there the night the queen showed up."

Kenny, who had been staring at his friend's performance, turned back to the painted face on the wall. That little frightened face—he had seen it somewhere before. Somewhere. . . .

And then like a bolt of lightning he remembered. It was the face he had seen at the window when they arrived at the castle!

4

B ut you must be mistaken, Kenny!" exclaimed Mrs. Spencer the next morning after her husband had left for the Auchterlony plant. "Are you trying to say there's a painting in the castle of the man you claim was at the window yesterday?"

Kenny nodded. "Duggie was with me when I spotted it. I'd know that scared little face anywhere." He hesitated. "I would have told Dad only I was afraid he might think I was really going off the deep end."

"I see," Nancy Spencer said quietly. "And this painting you saw yesterday. Did it say who it was?"

Kenny shifted his feet. It wasn't going to be easy. "The seventh Earl of Strathullen."

"The seventh Earl of Strathullen?" Mrs. Spencer looked stunned. She stared at her son, her eyes wide with concern. "But, Kenny! He's been dead since—since—"

"Since 1568."

She nodded. "I see, Kenny. And you saw him yesterday?" Her voice was just a little too casual.

He sighed. "Look, Mom, I'm not going crazy, if that's what you're thinking. I just know what I saw."

She put her arm around her son's shoulders and drew him to her. She spoke softly, in a wan, almost beseeching voice. "Look, Kenny, this is the first time you've ever lived in a house like this. It's a new experience for you. Each room has its own story to tell of the people who once lived here. In a sense, although they died years ago, they are *still* here. Their eyes stare down at us from their portraits. We touch the armor they wore, the swords and the lances they used in battle. Their very beds look as though they had been slept in only yesterday. And their books—" She laughed a little self-consciously.

"Remember, Kenny, when I thought that someone had been reading those books recently? Well, that's the very thing I'm talking about. When people find themselves in a strange, perhaps psychic, environment, their minds sometimes play tricks on them. Just the way your mind is playing tricks on you with this Earl of Strathullen business. You see, Kenny, it's—it's not *reasonable.*"

He was silent for a few moments. "I guess you're right, Mom," he conceded finally. "I mean, you've just got to be! The seventh Earl of Strathullen! Duggie says he must have been here the night the queen arrived after her escape from prison."

"I wonder what took place that night?" Mrs. Spencer mused as she let her eyes drift absently around the beamed dining room. "Why did she stay just the one night? Why—" She clamped her teeth and made a face. "There I go again, Kenny! Letting my fancy run wild! Doing the very thing I was accusing you of doing! Well, enough is enough. Let's talk about something else. How do you like Duggie Cameron?"

"A winner! Man, he's really something again! I still can't get over that private eye routine of his. By the way, he wanted to know if I'd ever been mugged in Central Park. I told him I'd never been mugged *anywhere.* Funny thing, but I had the feeling he was kind of disappointed. Like it was un-American of me not to have gotten myself mugged." He grinned. "Never expected to meet anyone like Duggie over here."

She nodded approvingly. "It just goes to show you can't stereotype people or nationalities. Like all the Scots are dour and all the English reserved. It just isn't so, thank goodness. Each of us is an individual—" She stopped, her face white in the sudden silence following a thud from somewhere in the castle. "What on earth was that?"

He shook his head. He had the feeling that the sound had come from somewhere in the great hall area. "Mrs. Wheerie?" he ventured.

"She's out."

"But—"

"We're the only ones here."

Kenny ran his tongue over his dry lips. There had to be an explanation for the noise they had just heard, only for some reason he wasn't too thrilled with the idea of finding out. He wasn't a coward but then he wasn't exactly a hero either. Finally he forced himself to his feet from the cane-backed chair on which he had been sitting. "I'll check. Be right back, Mom."

"No, Kenny, I'll—"

"You wait here. It's probably nothing."

He said the words more to reassure himself than his mother. He advanced from the dining room into the hall, his skin tight with apprehension. As his eyes traveled slowly around the huge chamber he could see that it was empty. Yet what had caused the noise they had just heard? He forced himself forward, his feet dragging on the smooth flagstones. As he passed the twin row of armored knights on the stairway, he experienced the sensation that someone was observing his every movement. Angrily he shook his head. Nerves! Just as his mother had been saying. Yet the feeling that unseen eyes were following him was still there when his mother joined him.

"Nothing," he said.

"But that noise—" All at once the note of concern left her voice and she laughed. "Look, Kenny! That big Lochaber ax over there. It must have slipped off the wall!"

"Huh?" Kenny wheeled around and stared wide eyed at the spot to which she was pointing. There on the ground lay a huge Lochaber battle-ax, the flagstone gouged where the sharp blade of the fearsome weapon had impacted. Kenny felt an enormous surge of relief as he crossed over to where the ax lay. So there *had* been a logical explanation for the noise they had heard! Why was he forever jumping at shadows!

"Good thing no one was around when it fell," opined Mrs. Spencer. She shivered slightly.

"Yeah," said Kenny thoughtfully. He lifted his

eyes to the spot, ten feet up the wall, where the ax had been secured. Now that was strange! The two heavy leather thongs did not look frayed or damaged in any way. And why were the metal buckles that had held the ax in place not engaged? Had someone deliberately released them? But why?

"Come along, Kenny," ordered his mother crisply. "At least we solved that mystery."

"Yeah," Kenny said again. He glanced uneasily around him. "Look, Mom, I'm not getting jumpy or anything like that. Honest. But you know, when I just came in here a moment ago, I had the weirdest feeling that I was being watched."

She said quietly, "That doesn't make sense."

He grunted. "Neither does something else. How that big neck chopper managed to fall off that wall." He forced a grin. "O.K., Mom, so I just happen to think this place is right out of Spookville. I'll bet the last owner was Count Dracula. No wonder Mary Queen of Scots only stayed one night before she split. The old gal smelled a rat."

Mrs. Spencer seemed relieved at the direction the conversation had taken. "Actually Mary was just a young woman then. I've been reading about her in the library. Strange the number of books there are in the castle about her. Somebody here must have found her awfully interesting. Anyway,

Mary had a tragic life, I'm afraid. Tragic death, too." She linked her arm through her son's. "Now, why don't you run over to Duggie's place? I've got heaps of work to do. Mr. Budlong will be here tomorrow from California. The first sales meeting will be held right in this hall. I've got a zillion things to take care of and I'm afraid Mrs. Wheerie may be a little late in returning. She said she'd be looking in at the cemetery. Her husbands are buried there."

Kenny grinned sourly. "If she's gonna be looking in on all four of them, she could be tied up for the rest of the day." He made his way to the front door, then hesitated. "If you think I could help—" he began in a voice bereft of enthusiasm.

"Thanks, but you'd just be in the way. Incidentally, I've also got a number of errands to take care of later. Use your key if Mrs. Wheerie hasn't come back from the cemetery."

Duggie Cameron lived in a small sandstone cottage on the outskirts of Auchterlony. Kenny had no difficulty in finding it, but was disappointed to learn when he got there that Duggie had accompanied his father on a brief business trip. Leaving the cottage, Kenny wandered morosely along a deserted High Street, which apparently served as the main thoroughfare in the village. It couldn't have been more than twenty feet across and it took Kenny only ten minutes to exhaust whatever charms it had. The only building of any size was a squat red-brick affair which he recognized as the home of Fraser's Creamy Toffee.

He swung to the rear of the factory and found himself on a narrow cobblestoned lane that led off into the glen beyond the little town. He hesitated. There didn't seem to be very much doing beyond Auchterlony. On the other hand, he had already established that there wasn't very much doing *in* Auchterlony. He shrugged and followed his footsteps along the hawthorn-hedged lane that seemed to wander off in every direction. He had been strolling along, indifferent to where the lane might be taking him, when he rounded a blind bend and found himself face to face with what appeared to be the ruins of an ancient church.

He stared in wonder at the great mound of blackened stone that must at one time have been an imposing edifice. From the few arches and pillars that remained, it was obvious to him that this had been no typical village kirk serving a poor, pastoral community. Curious, he made his way up to an iron gate that marked the entrance to what was left of the building. There was a crudely lettered sign on the gate and Kenny had difficulty in reading the inscription.

THE ANCIENT CHAPEL OF ST. FILLAN
AND FINAL RESTING-PLACE
OF THE EARLS OF STRATHULLEN

Kenny found the burial grounds without any trouble. The small cemetery lay just beyond the

nave of the church. For some reason, the cemetery was not as weed-and-nettle strewn as the church, and apparently someone must have tended the burial grounds from time to time. Each grave, he noted, was marked by a granite obelisk which recorded in simple terms the dates and titles of the various earls and the place of death. There was a severe absence of Latin epitaphs and Biblical injunctions on the stones. It was as though the stern Earls of Strathullen had been impatient to get the whole business of interment completed with the least delay and be allowed to rest.

Kenny paused when he arrived at the last of the graves. He had thought that all of them were alike. The same-sized obelisks. The same absence of sentiment on the stones. The same iron chain that enclosed each plot. Yet it was clear as he stood beside the last grave that they were not all alike. While grass and tiny wildflowers bloomed on the others, the grave of the seventh Earl of Strathullen was completely barren. Only the harsh earth showed, sere and brown, seemingly devoid of life. Bemused for a reason he could not have explained, Kenny took one final look around the churchyard, then made his way home.

His mother was gone when he got there, and apparently Mrs. Wheerie was still at the cemetery as no one answered his ring. After a moment's hesitation, Kenny got out his key and let himself in. It was cool in the great hall and he noted that, since he had left, a long table had been set up for the meeting with Homer Budlong. No doubt his father had sent over a few workmen from the factory because a supply of pens and writing pads had been placed on the conference table, as well as place-names.

He crossed over to the kitchen and helped himself to a glass of milk and some biscuits and cheese. It was still as death in the castle and he suddenly found himself wishing for the sound of another human—even if it were only Mrs. Wheerie. The scrape of his shoes on the flagstones echoed in his ears, almost as though someone were following at his heels. Nerves! There it was again! He was letting his imagination take over. Well, enough was enough!

The Lochaber ax was still on the ground where it had fallen. Glowering at it, Kenny suddenly saw in it everything that had upset him since arriving at Strathullen Castle. With a grunt he drew back his right foot and lashed out viciously at the ax. He let out a howl as his shoe came in contact with the solid object on the ground. Groaning with pain, he hopped frantically around on his undamaged foot until the pain slowly subsided. The

Lochaber ax hadn't budged from where it lay and he drew back his foot again before thinking better of it.

"Clever lad," said a gentle voice from somewhere behind him.

Kenny spun around and gaped in astonishment at the speaker. He was small and he was wearing a kilt with dark green and blue squares and thin white stripes. A Balmoral bonnet with an eagle feather perched on his head. From his right stocking protruded a fierce *sgian-dubh,* the Highland dirk so deadly in hand-to-hand combat. A curved sword hung in its scabbard from the stranger's waist.

But it was not the costume, strange as it was, that riveted all of Kenny's shocked attention. It was the face. A face so pale and lean that the light from the window appeared to be seeping *through* it! The eyes were dark and deep set, and the young American had the feeling that he had seen them somewhere before. He was frightened and he had to jerk his jaw muscles twice to unhinge the words. Even then they came out small and cramped.

"What are you doing here?" he finally managed.

The stranger shrugged under his blue satin doublet. "Why now, and I live here," he returned mildly. His voice had an odd up-and-down lilt to it that Kenny found difficult to place. The accent seemed quaint and not at all like the accent of the Scots Kenny had met so far.

"You live here—?" Kenny began. Something was wrong. Horribly wrong. No one had lived in Strathullen Castle for a hundred years. And that face—

"Who are you?"

The little man seemed to hesitate. "I was never one for formalities, lad. It would suit me fine if you just call me Mr. MacDhu."

"Mr. MacDhu?" repeated the boy. He was sure he had heard the name recently, only where? He sucked in his breath as memory pressed a button in his mind. The name on the painting he had seen with Duggie!

His skin seemed to tighten against his bones as he waited in the awful stillness for the stranger to speak.

"They also call me the seventh Earl of Strathullen," said the little man in the kilt.

Kenny's voice was the merest whisper. "But—but he—you—have been dead for four hundred years . . ." He did not finish the sentence.

"Yes," said the stranger.

✹ 5

They stood quite still. The man with the gentle
smile. The boy with the frightened eyes. The
word just spoken by the stranger seemed to trem-
ble in the air.

Kenny opened his mouth. No cry came out. He
wanted to run but his legs seemed rooted to the
ground. He shrank back against the wall, away
from the battle-ax at his feet, away from the soft-
spoken man in the odd Highland costume. Fear,
like no fear he had ever known, swept through his
body in ice-cold flashes.

The stranger must have guessed the boy's panic
for he withdrew a few steps, an expression of con-
trition on his face. "Och, but I frightened you, lad!

This stupid sword and dagger, I suppose. They're all show, really. Like everything else about me."

The words that Kenny spoke were hardly words at all. Only a trembling movement of his frozen lips. "You are the seventh Earl of Strathullen?"

"Aye, the same."

"But—but just an hour ago I saw your grave." Kenny swallowed both his heart and his words. After a long silence he continued. "It said you were buried there a long time ago—"

Mr. MacDhu smiled. "October 20, 1568, to be exact. A man should always remember the date he died. After all, now, it's just as important to him as the day he was born, is it no?"

Kenny said nothing. There was nothing to say.

"So you're wondering no doubt why I happen to be here and not in the little kirkyard of St. Fillan, is that it? Well, there has to be a logical explanation for it, eh? And do you know what that explanation is? I'm a ghost."

"Oh," said Kenny.

"I mean I have to be *something.*"

"Of course," returned the boy. He caught the look of distress on Mr. MacDhu's face. "A ghost," he said. It was unreal. The whole thing couldn't be happening to him. Only it was. "But nobody believes in ghosts today—"

Mr. MacDhu looked hurt. "*I* do."

"Well, that's because you are one," Kenny blurted out without thinking. He knew he had said the wrong thing and hurried on. "I mean, if you died four hundred years ago—"

"I have to be something," concluded Mr. MacDhu, "just as I said. I'm not in my grave, but I'm here. If I wasn't here I'd be in my grave. It's just good Scots logic."

"It was you I saw at the window—"

"Aye, myself. I was wondering what all the commotion was. I've been here all by myself since that daft old woman fell from the balcony. What was her name, now?"

"Nell Dalhousie."

"Aye, that was it." Mr. MacDhu's face darkened. "Always creeping around in that long nightgown with a candle in her hand. Scared me half to death, she did."

Maybe it was the idea of a ghost being afraid of an old lady that brought back Kenny's courage. "So you've lived here all your life, Mr. MacDhu?"

"All my life and a bit longer." The stranger chuckled as though he had just delivered a rare witticism. "It's the peace and quiet of Strathullen that I love. No one to bother me at all. Until now." He paused, cocked his head, and studied the boy.

"You have a queer way of talking, aye, and that's for certain. Where are you from, now?"

"Me? Connecticut." He suddenly realized that if Mr. MacDhu had died in 1568 he might not know where Connecticut was. "That's in America."

"America?" The little ghost looked shocked. "I thought they were all savages over there."

"Only some of us," Kenny returned politely. "My father was transferred to Auchterlony. His company bought Fraser's Creamy Toffee. They have to use the castle for a lot of the office work."

Mr. MacDhu wrung his pale hands. "But this is terrible! After all, this is my castle! It belongs to the Earls of Strathullen who were the chiefs of the great Clan MacDhu!" He glowered at Kenny. "What's the name of the clan that's invading my castle?"

"Well, it's not really a clan. That is unless you call a bunch of businessmen a clan. United Groceries Holdings, it's called. Mom calls it UGH for short."

"UGH for short," repeated Mr. MacDhu. "They deserve a name like that." He removed his Highland bonnet and smoothed the eagle feather that signified his rank as head of his clan. "And their chieftain?"

Kenny frowned. "If you mean the top honcho

69

then that would have to be Homer M. Budlong. He's the one who bought Fraser's Toffee."

The little ghost nodded as he returned his bonnet to his head. His face was thoughtful. "Queer now. I never met the man, yet already I hate him. Of all the places on earth he could have gone to, why did he have to come to *my* castle? Aye, and without even a by-your-leave." He shook his head sorrowfully, then suddenly seemed to think of something. "Your name, lad? You haven't told me your name?"

"Kenny. Kenny Spencer."

Mr. MacDhu grunted. "Just as long as it's no Homer M. Budlong!" He scowled as he adjusted the leather sporran on his kilt. "Look, Kenny, I like you, and it's not that I have anything against you colonists or whatever you call yourselves nowadays, but dash it all, it's my castle! I never invited this Homer M. Budlong to make toffee here!"

Kenny shrugged. "Then toss him out. He'll be here tomorrow for the big sales meeting."

"Toss him out?" repeated Mr. MacDhu. There was an anguished expression on his face. "But you don't understand, lad! Me—in a common brawl—" He shuddered.

"Look, Mr. MacDhu, I've been noticing the

paintings of your ancestors. They're all over this place. Real mean-looking guys, with their straggly beards and broken noses. Those dudes must have played rough and mean. And they were all Mac-Dhus."

"True enough," said the small ghost with a sigh. "But alas, I was always different from the others. You see before you the one who brought eternal disgrace to a proud family. The single coward in the once mighty Clan MacDhu." He brushed what might have been a tear from his eyes. "And that is the reason that I haunt these grounds. I am an outcast, a pariah, cursed for my cowardice to the grave, aye, and beyond."

Kenny had long since lost his last vestige of fear. The crushed face of the little man in front of him was too pathetic. Too sorrowful. The very finery that he wore, the brave tartan, the chief's crest on his bonnet, seemed to mock him as a creature of no worth. Kenny could not deny the wash of pity that flooded his heart. On an impulse he blurted out, "But how *did* you become a ghost, Mr. MacDhu? And why only you of all your clan?"

"That is a secret," Mr. MacDhu returned stiffly. "A secret too shameful to tell. A black secret."

"Oh," said Kenny. He was sorry he had brought the matter up, for the seventh Earl of Strathullen had a wild look in his eyes and his bony fingers seemed to be tightening around the handle of his sword. "None of my business," he added hastily. "Don't want to be nosy."

Mr. MacDhu was staring off into space. Clearly he hadn't heard what Kenny had just said. And apparently he had come to a decision about something. "Och, now, and maybe it will no be mattering greatly after all these years. Aye, and perhaps my story will be helpful to you, lad. My story of cowardice and eternal shame."

There was something so intense about his face that Kenny felt it prudent to retreat a few steps. "As I said, I couldn't care less how you became a ghost. Honest. Just forget I even asked. O.K.?"

"Forget?" A bitter smile bent the bloodless lips. "And how can one forget? The scars are too deep. The pain too insistent. The memory too fresh. No, I will tell you my story. Tell you it in all its horror. But not now. Let us say the day after tomorrow. I must have time to go over in my mind the events of that awful night in 1568. The night Mary Queen of Scots fled to this house hotly pursued by her enemies. Let us meet in the room upstairs where my picture hangs. I call it my blue room, the room where I first saw the light of day." He shook his head mournfully. "Alas, that it might have been myself hanging there and not a mere portrait."

Kenny edged farther back. He didn't like the smoldering fire in the eyes of the little Highlander. "Like I said, Mr. MacDhu, you don't have to bother. Besides, I'm going to be awfully busy—"

Mr. MacDhu stayed him with an upraised hand. "I have given you my word," he said firmly. "The word of a MacDhu is no given lightly. Aye, and once it is given there can be no changing it. The day after tomorrow. Before midday. Until then— go in peace."

"But Mr. MacDhu—" Kenny cried, then stopped. He stared, his eyes wide with horror. Something was happening to Mr. MacDhu! He appeared to be caught up in a fine mist that seemed to be rising from the ground. Already his buckled shoes were growing dim. And then all at once Kenny couldn't see them any more. They were followed a moment later by the little man's bare knees and the leather sporran, that acted as a purse. Now there was only half of Mr. MacDhu visible, the top half, and it seemed to be floating gently in space. Kenny opened his mouth, then swallowed whatever words he had been about to utter. Somehow there seemed no point in talking to only half of him. Besides, even that was slowly disappearing before Kenny's eyes until only the top of the Highland bonnet remained. It drifted eerily up the stairway as though borne on a current of air and then, before Kenny quite realized what had happened, it too was gone.

The boy stood motionless in the vast hall, like one emerging from a trance. He was conscious of a sense of confusion, of unreality. Could he have dreamed the whole thing? No, it had been too vivid, too intense. But a 400-year-old ghost? And one living in the same house? It was just too preposterous.

He had almost convinced himself that he had imagined the whole scene when he suddenly noticed the feather on the ground.

And he knew in his heart it could only have fallen from the Highland bonnet of Mr. MacDhu, the seventh Earl of Strathullen.

6

Mrs. Wheerie, in her customary black dress, was in the kitchen when he got there. Apparently she had let herself in through a side entrance while he was in the great hall. It was obvious to Kenny that her visit to the cemetery had improved her spirits for she was humming softly as he entered. True, the tune she was endeavoring to carry with indifferent success seemed to be some kind of old Scots hymn, for it was slow and lugubrious. Still, she was clearly somewhat less solemn and reserved than when he had last seen her.

"I'm sorry if I'm a wee bit late," she confided as she prepared a salad. "I had to tidy up the graves in the cemetery. I wouldn't want any o' my husbands to be jealous o' the others. They were equal in life, aye, and if it's up to me they'll be equal in death. Each has his own tombstone with his own name on it." She looked almost smug. "There's no many can claim as much."

"Gosh, that's really something, Mrs. Wheerie." He hoped he didn't sound too much like a hypocrite.

"Some widows around Auchterlony are no like me. They would have used the one stone and squeezed in the names o' the others. I'm no like that. If a man's good enough to be my husband, he's good enough to have his ain tombstone."

"Right," said Kenny. She was humming again and he hoped there would be no more talk about death. Clearly it was a subject that fascinated the housekeeper. He thought it better to speak of something else. "By the way, Mrs. Wheerie, I understand that a lot of these old Scottish castles have a ghost in them. Or so some people say. Is that true?"

She looked at him quickly, her eyes suddenly wary. "Och, and it's just daft gossip, lad. Don't you believe a word o' it. There's no bogles around here."

"Including Strathullen Castle?" he pressed.

"Including Strathullen Castle!" she returned almost harshly. After a long silence she continued on a softer note. "That face you thought you saw at the window frightened you, is that the way o' it? Well, I'm sure there was nothing to it. Nothing at all. Besides, would a clever man like Mr. Budlong now buy himself a castle with a bogle in it?" What may have been a smile bent the severe lips. "You worry ower much for a lad. Run along now. Have you seen the grounds around the castle? My, but they're grand! The finest in all the Highlands, I'm thinking. And here's a bannock and some cheese for you."

A lot of thoughts twisted and turned in Kenny's mind as he made his way between the twin rows of yew hedges beyond the castle walls. Why was Mrs. Wheerie at such pains to say there was no ghost in Strathullen Castle? Why did the very subject of ghosts seem to upset her? And come to think of it, she must have been in the kitchen when he met Mr. MacDhu. She had a way of moving soundlessly from room to room. Could she possibly have seen or heard anything? If she had, she'd made no mention of it. Still, that should scarcely have been surprising, considering her secretive ways.

He sighed as he crossed a small garden bordered by brilliant masses of rhododendron and hydrangea. To think it had only been a day or so ago that he had been feeling sorry for himself in dull, humdrum old Scotland where nothing ever happened!

Nothing, that is, unless you wanted to exclude the likes of an inscrutable housekeeper who just happened to have buried four husbands.

And a 400-year-old ghost who haunted the house where you lived.

7

The following day Homer Budlong flew in from California to preside over the first meeting of Fraser's Creamy Toffee to be held since the take-over. Trailed by a thin, nervous man laden with briefcases, Budlong burst into the castle as though he had been propelled from a siege gun. Without a moment's hesitation he headed into the great hall, took over the chair at the head of the conference table, grunted, then thrust a cigar into his mouth. He waited, expressionless, while the nervous assistant hastily dropped his briefcases and produced a light for the cigar.

The president of United Groceries Holdings was a powerful, barrel-chested man whose tough,

heavily fleshed face suggested two things: That he
loved to eat, and that he loved to fight. It was by a
judicious merger of the two that he had risen to
his present preeminent position in the fast-food
and produce business. Now with sales booming nationally, the big conglomerate was looking abroad
for new markets and new products. That was the
reason UGH had snapped up Fraser's, a conserva-
tive little company that had been making toffee

for over a hundred years. It was a natural for the booming California corporation, and Homer Budlong meant to make the most of it. His shrewd eyes traveled around the long table where his executives were gathered. As his attention was fixed solely on the business at hand, he did not notice the two boys who were observing everything from behind the armored knights on the stairway.

"That's him," whispered Kenny. "Homer M. Budlong. The beefy character with the bald head and the cigar. Dad says he's Mr. Big in the fast-food business."

Duggie grinned as he studied the girth of the man at the head of the table. "Mr. Big is right. He looks like he eats more than he sells."

"Sh! Keep your voice low, Duggie! If Dad ever knew I was here he'd skin me alive." Kenny peered out cautiously from his place of concealment. "I think they're getting ready."

Homer Budlong removed his cigar from his mouth and waited for the murmur of voices and rustle of papers to die away. Assured he had everyone's attention, he coughed as though testing the timber of his voice. "Good morning and welcome to our first meeting. They tell me that Strathullen Castle has a lot of tradition behind it, and so of course does Fraser's Creamy Toffee. I guess you might say they were made for each other."

"Right on, H.M.," chirped the nervous assistant.

Budlong ignored him. His thoughts seemed far away as his eyes drifted curiously around the great hall. "Strange sort of place," he murmured, as though speaking to himself. "Not many places like this in California." He suddenly frowned. "What the devil are all those big axes doing up there on the wall? Looks like they're getting ready for a woodchoppers ball."

Ian Cameron, the Works' Manager, glanced around and smiled. "Oh, those, Homer? They're Lochaber battle-axes. In the old days when the castle was under siege the Earls of Strathullen would grab them and repel the invaders."

For a reason that puzzled Kenny, peering from his hiding place, Homer Budlong seemed greatly interested in the words just spoken. "Really, Ian? So these are genuine Lochaber axes, eh? Funny, I would never have thought them so large. Must have taken a real man to wield one." There was admiration in his voice, his eyes. "Yep, they must have been real scrappers, those old clansmen. My kind of guys in more ways than one. As a matter of fact, did I ever tell you that—"

"Cablegram for you, Mr. Budlong." It was one

of the secretaries who interrupted him. She waited until he dismissed her with a wave of his cigar.

Homer Budlong grunted as his small eyes swept over the message. "My itinerary for the next two weeks. They get panicky in Beverly Hills when I'm on the road." He crammed the cablegram into his pocket. "Well, that's life, as the old cliché has it."

"Well put, H.M.," contributed the assistant, bobbing his head in enthusiastic agreement. "Well put, indeed."

"Enough, Hepplewaithe," said Budlong without bothering to look at him. He filled his glass with water, then took a slow sip, for all the world like a connoisseur sampling some rare vintage wine. He ran his tongue thoughtfully over his upper lip and turned to Duggie's father. "Excellent water you have here, Ian. Some people think that all drinking water is the same. That's because they have no sense of taste. They couldn't tell a pizza from a hamburger. Now this water has strong characteristics. It's vigorous, yet it isn't pushy. It's smooth, yet it isn't bland. Maybe we ought to think of putting it in bottles and selling it as it is."

Jim Spencer grinned. "Scotch water? Hey, that would be a switch. Think what they're charging for Scotch whiskey! After all, it's just a matter of taste."

Homer Budlong moved his big head in vigorous agreement. He pounded the table with a huge fist. "Right, Jim! Taste! That's the name of the game! That's what the food business is all about. First the product, then the package, then the promotion." He scowled at the man with the nervous smile seated across the way from him. "You got that, Hepplewaithe?"

The assistant smiled even more nervously as he scribbled furiously on a yellow pad. "Got it, H.M. The product, the package, the promotion."

Homer Budlong jammed his cigar into a corner of his mouth and talked around it. "I hope you've got it, Hepplewaithe. I don't like to repeat myself. That is, unless I've said something very clever." He chuckled, waited for Hepplewaithe to chuckle also, then rapped the table for attention. "Well, let's get on with business. We'll retain the Fraser name, of course. It's a sound, Scottish name and helps identify the product." He removed the cigar from his mouth and his fingers strayed absently to the platter of Scottish delicacies that Mrs. Wheerie had prepared for the meeting. He frowned at one of the pastries. "What the devil is this?"

Duggie's father glanced at the object in question and smiled. "That one? That's called a Forfar Bridie. It's like a meat pancake. Very popular over here."

Budlong stared at it warily, sniffed it, then sank his teeth into it. He chewed reflectively, eyes closed, a look of intense concentration under the beetling brows. "Diced beef," he muttered. "Chopped onions. Pepper. And some kind of paste—" He took another bite.

He said no more until the Forfar Bridie was gone. Then he turned to Mr. Spencer. His voice trembled with emotion. "This is a work of art! Where on earth did you get it?"

"Mrs. Wheerie made these. She's the housekeeper."

"Housekeeper! The woman is an artist! A virtuoso!" He suddenly frowned. "Mrs. Wheerie? Yes, I remember now. I hired her in Auchterlony at the take-over. Extraordinary woman. I sensed then that she had a unique talent." He paused. "Well, I think it's time we got back to our agenda."

Hepplewaithe whipped out a fresh yellow pad. "Anytime you're ready, H.M."

Budlong looked at him, wrinkled his big beak of a nose, and grunted. "Now the thing we have to remember is that anybody can make a bar of toffee. What we have to concentrate on is how to promote Fraser's. We've got to find out what's different about our toffee. In other words, as they say on Madison Avenue, we've got to find the deceptive differential. Then flog the competition to death with it."

Jim Spencer exchanged a puzzled look with Ian Cameron, then turned to his boss. "I don't get to New York too often. Mind explaining what the ad boys on Madison Avenue mean by deceptive differential?"

The president grinned. "Got you, huh? Well, it's no big deal. Everything in the fast-food line is the same today. Hot dogs, fried chicken, you name it. All made of the same garbage. One pizza tastes like any other pizza. Blah and double blah. What we have to zero in on is the one thing that makes Fraser's toffee different from everybody else's toffee." His eyes hooded and his voice went silky soft. "Even if it really *isn't* different."

Jim Spencer said "Mm," and tugged thoughtfully at his ear. "The deceptive differential. I see what you mean. Only what's different about toffees? They're all made from butter, sugar, fats, milk—" He stopped and snapped his fingers. "Highland milk!"

"Exactly!" Homer Budlong's voice was a small purr of triumph. "Highland milk! So who cares if

Highland milk is better or worse than any other kind? We'll be the only ones who have it. And remember, we're not just selling a product. We're selling a concept as well. And now to flavors."

"Flavors?" Ian Cameron frowned. "Fraser's has only got one flavor, Homer. The one old Andrew Fraser came up with a hundred years ago."

"Ian," said Homer Budlong solemnly, "suppose Howard Johnson had only one ice cream flavor? Or Wrigley one chewing gum flavor? They'd be dead!" He stared hard across the table. "Right, Hepplewaithe?"

The assistant, who had been scribbling furiously, looked up from his pad. "Right, H.M. One chewing gum flavor. Got it."

"One crummy flavor. That's all Fraser's ever had. A hundred years of the same goo. I tried it. It tasted like heather and axle grease." He crashed his fist down on the table. "Flavors! We've got to give the public what it wants! Raspberry—cinnamon—tutti-frutti—" He paused, breathing hard, then threw out his arm dramatically. "Men, a whole toffee world is lying at our feet out there, infinite, boundless. Like Cortez on that peak in Darien when he discovered the Pacific—" His voice trailed away and a glazed look came into his eyes as he stared off into the distance. With a grunt, he snapped out of the trance that had held him. "Where was I, Hepplewaithe?"

The flustered assistant referred to his notes and cleared his throat. "You were on some peak in Darien, H.M., discovering the Pacific."

Budlong glared at him, then turned to Jim Spencer. "Remember the name of the game is hype! Get going on jingles and catchy slogans for the radio. 'Fraser's, the toffier toffee'—stuff like that."

Jim Spencer groaned slightly and looked away from Ian Cameron who was smiling.

"So that's it, men," concluded Budlong feelingly as he gazed around the table. "This is the big league now. This is Broadway on opening night. Superbowl Sunday and the seventh day of the World Series. We do a good psyche job on ourselves and we pick up all the marbles." Again he wheeled around to Kenny's father. "Well, that's the game plan, Jim. I'm giving you the football on your own two-yard line. You've got the whole field ahead but I know you're gonna score big. And don't forget, you've got me and Hepplewaithe running interference!"

Jim Spencer glanced doubtfully at the nervous assistant whose pen was racing across his yellow pad. Whatever thoughts were passing through his mind at the moment, he kept them to himself. "Sure," he said.

Homer Budlong got to his feet, then frowned as his eyes traveled over the great hall of the castle. "You know something? I've got a hunch we ought to get rid of some of the old junk lying around here. The place looks like a medieval used-car lot. And all those beat-up old flags hanging up there! Like it was laundry day in Jersey City." He glanced at his watch. "Three o'clock already? I'm supposed to be in Geneva in three hours!" He scooped up his briefcase and a handful of papers. "Let's go, Hepplewaithe—" He never finished the sentence for the next moment, as Kenny and Duggie peered from their hiding place, a scream burst from his lips.

Jim Spencer was the first to recover. "Homer? Are you all right?"

Budlong's face was as white as the papers clutched in his hand. His lips trembled. "Just now. I felt it. A hand. A hand cold as ice. It touched my neck. The fingers were small, like a child's, and clammy. Then they started crawling—" He shuddered. There were beads of perspiration on his forehead.

Jim Spencer frowned and stared at where his boss had been sitting. "A clammy hand? Like a child's? But no one was near you!"

"Maybe a current of air," suggested Duggie's father. "These old castles are like that. Drafty—"

"A hand," intoned Homer Budlong solemnly. "Clammy as death and cold as ice."

"Clammy as death and cold as ice," droned the nervous man across the table, still scribbling.

"Enough, Hepplewaithe!" snapped Budlong. He was silent for a long moment, then turned to Duggie's father. "I suppose you're right, Ian. It had to be a draft of some kind. Strange though. . . ." He shook his head.

"Can we get you to the airport?" Jim Spencer asked.

"No need. We've got our limousine waiting outside. Let's go, Hepplewaithe. They're waiting for us in Geneva." He shook hands quickly with Jim Spencer and Ian Cameron, waved his briefcase at the others, then strode with quick, purposeful strides toward the door. It was a dramatic exit. Kenny, crouched alongside Duggie, had to admit that. It would have been an even more dramatic one if the forward progress of the quick, purposeful strides hadn't come to an abrupt halt just as Homer Budlong came abreast of where the

boys lay hidden. With a suddenness that froze the
air in Kenny's lungs, the big man's feet shot out
from under him. The next moment, still holding
onto his briefcase as though it were some sort of
lifeline, Homer Budlong went soaring through the
air before landing with a loud thud on the flag-
stoned floor of Strathullen Castle. Throwing cau-

tion to the wind and caught up in the frenzy of the moment, Kenny burst from his place of concealment. He was the first to reach the spot where Homer Budlong lay holding his bald head and groaning loudly.

"Are you all right, Mr. Budlong?" he exclaimed anxiously.

"Eh? Of course I'm not all right! Why should I be all right when I just cracked my skull on this stupid floor?" The man glared furiously around him as he struggled to his feet. "Somebody tripped me! Lifted the feet right from underneath me!"

Jim Spencer's face was grim as he regarded his son. "What are you doing here, Kenny? This is a management meeting. I just hope you have a good explanation."

It was Duggie who saved the day. His face was a parchment of innocence as he answered. "It was my fault, Mr. Spencer. I asked Kenny if we could go to the kitchen for one of Mrs. Wheerie's Forfar Bridies. We could see the meeting was going on and we didn't want to get in the way. That's why we were sneaking around here, hoping you wouldn't see us. Of course, when Mr. Budlong fell, we just had to help. We just thought it was the right thing to do. Even if it meant getting a licking for being where we weren't supposed to be."

Kenny stared with awe and admiration at the

redheaded youngster with the Western shirt and the cowboy boots. The guileless expression on Duggie Cameron's face would have melted a heart of stone. Homer Budlong didn't have a chance.

"Forget why the kids are here. They're O.K." The president of UGH dabbed at his bald head with a handkerchief. "What I want to know is, who tripped me?"

"Who?" Jim Spencer looked startled. "But you were all by yourself when you fell. There wasn't a soul near you."

"And yet somebody tripped me," Homer Budlong said ominously. "I distinctly felt a foot. Funny thing, but it seemed small, with some weird kind of buckle—" His voice trailed off into silence.

Ian Cameron looked at him oddly. "Well, the main thing is that you're all right, Homer. I still think it was one of those uneven flagstones. Notice how they're cracked in some places?"

"So is my head," snapped the Californian. His eyes drifted moodily around the hall. "Creepy sort of place," he muttered. He seemed puzzled about something. Finally, he shook his head as though mustering his thoughts. "Where were we, Hepplewaithe, before all this happened?"

Hepplewaithe glanced at his yellow pad. "You were on your way to Geneva, H.M."

Homer Budlong nodded. He did not seem quite

as sure of himself as before. He walked with slow, deliberate steps to the door. He turned when he got there and stared back at the hall. At the motionless banners that hung from the rafters. At the battle-axes and swords and the helmeted knights standing at attention at the foot of the marble stairway. "Creepy," he said again. "Nothing like this in Beverly Hills." The next moment, followed by Hepplewaithe, he was gone.

"Well," murmured Ian Cameron after a long moment of silence, "what was that all about?"

Jim Spencer shook his head. There was a thoughtful expression on his face. "Beats me. First a clammy hand, small, like a child's. Next a buckled shoe. . . ."

94

8

Duggie's eyes narrowed. "Somebody in the castle? You saw the guy, Kenny?" It was a few hours after the sales meeting and the boys were making their way across the heather-flecked glen just beyond the village. It was a scene of somber desolation as far as the eye could see, the only evidence of life the raucous scolding of a stonechat from a nearby thicket.

Kenny nodded reluctantly. He had been hesitant about telling Duggie, fearful that his new friend might treat the whole thing as some kind of far-out joke. Still, he had to tell someone about his meeting with Mr. MacDhu, and if not Duggie, who else? He could scarcely confide in his mother and

95

father. They would surely think he had flipped. So, by the process of elimination, that left Duggie. Just the same it wasn't going to be easy.

"He was a little guy. He was wearing a kilt of some clan tartan I've never seen before. He said his name was MacDhu."

"MacDhu?" Duggie looked at him sharply. "That was the clan name of the Earls of Strathullen. There hasn't been a MacDhu around Auchterlony or Glen Arley in years."

"Well, there's one here now and he lives in the castle." He paused. "Actually he claims to be the seventh Earl of Strathullen."

Duggie stared at him. "Somebody's trying to play games with you! The guy you're talking about died in 1568. His body is buried in the Chapel of St. Fillan."

Kenny sifted the words carefully in his mind. It wasn't going to be easy to find the right ones. "Actually, Duggie, it's not his body in the castle. It's his ghost."

"Ghost?" Duggie's jaw dropped. "You saw a ghost?"

"And talked with him. Nice little fellow."

"Nice little fellow," repeated Duggie grimly. "Look, Kenny, I hate to be the one to tell you this, but you're nuts! Ghosts don't exist. They're not scientific." He moved his shoulders in a shrug. "Anyway, you must have seen and spoken to someone. Why don't you start from the beginning and tell me everything that happened? I warn you though, I'm a tough hombre to convince when it comes to ghosts."

Despite his outward show of cynicism, Duggie listened without interruption and with mounting interest as Kenny told his story. He was silent after the American had finished, a bemused expression on his face.

"So what do you think?" Kenny asked impatiently.

"Mrs. Wheerie," he said softly. "Where does she fit into all of this? It was right after her last husband died that she suddenly applied for the caretaker's job. She would check out the castle a few times a week to see that everything was in order." He frowned. "You felt she was trying to hide something. But why would she want to do that?"

"Forget Mrs. Wheerie. What about Mr. MacDhu?"

Duggie hesitated. "Probably a tinker. I'm not sure."

"A tinker? What's a tinker?"

"They're like gypsies here in Scotland. You see them all over the countryside with their knock-kneed little Highland ponies selling pots and pans. They live by their wits. Real sharpies. This dude you met has probably worked some sort of deal with Mrs. Wheerie. No doubt he made some payoff to her and she arranged to have him live rent free in the castle. It was a nice setup until Budlong took over the place and loused up their little racket. And by the way, it explains why Mrs. Wheerie didn't want you talking about having seen someone in the castle. She was afraid you had spotted her pal."

Kenny grunted. "Nice figuring, Duggie, only you forget one thing. Mr. MacDhu's face is exactly the same as the face on the painting we both saw."

Duggie affected a pained look. "What does that mean? Zilch! Look, these tinkers are sharp like razors. He probably got one of his pals to knock off a cheap painting of him. Just in case he needed some kind of proof he was the MacDhu he claimed to be."

"But his outfit! His kilt with that odd clan tartan, and that Highland bonnet with the crazy feather."

"Rented, most likely. Sauchiehall Street in Glasgow has loads of places where you can get yourself dressed up to look like Bonnie Prince Charlie's uncle. Anyway, I'm pretty sure Mrs. Wheerie and this guy are in cahoots in whatever is going on." He rubbed his nose reflectively. "Interesting case. Certain novel elements I haven't run across before." He made a few entries in a black notebook. "Of course there will be no charge for my services."

Kenny stared at him. "I'm not giving you any case, Duggie Cameron! I just thought I could confide in you—"

"Exactly," interrupted Duggie. He patted his friend reassuringly on the shoulder. "The way I see this case you're going to need all the professional help you can get. Meanwhile, if I were you, I wouldn't say too much around the village."

Kenny grunted. "You think I'm crazy? Tell someone we live in a haunted house? Who's gonna believe me?"

"After what happened to him today, I know someone who just might."

"Who?"

Duggie grinned. "Homer M. Budlong."

Mr. MacDhu was waiting for Kenny when the boy got to the meeting place the next day. He was dressed as Kenny had last seen him. The little man nodded his satisfaction as Kenny entered the room with the blue tapestries.

"So it's yourself! I've been a wee bit afraid you might have lost your courage after what happened at that meeting yesterday. Still I had to do something. Did you just hear that big loudmouth with the cigar! What was his name again?"

"Budlong. Homer M. Budlong."

"Budlong." Mr. MacDhu frowned, apparently lost in thought. "Strange," he mused. "I've just met the man, yet I have the feeling I've known him all my life. That chin, that big beaked nose, that voice—" He did not finish the sentence. Finally he shrugged. "Anyway, that man will be thinking twice before he sneers at my castle again! Aye, and did you hear him, lad? Comparing our MacDhu flags with dirty laundry! Well, he won't do that again!"

Kenny said nothing. So it had been the little ghost after all! The small clammy hand, and the buckled shoe that had sent Mr. Budlong flying through the air. But then he had hardly doubted that in some way Mr. MacDhu had been behind everything that had happened.

"Well, Kenny, let us go on to other matters. Two

days ago you asked me how it was I became the ghost you see before you. It was not an easy question to answer and I have been turning over in my mind since then how best to tell you. For I see now that my shame must be openly confessed. Too long I have kept it secret. Aye, far too long." He waved Kenny to a chair.

The boy backed away uneasily. He did not like the direction the talk was taking. "Look, Mr. MacDhu, you don't really have to tell me anything. It's none of my business. You don't pry into my affairs. I don't pry—"

"Sit!" Mr. MacDhu said firmly. His brow was dark and there was a strange light in his eyes. Kenny gulped, reached for the chair, and sat. Small and frail Mr. MacDhu might be but there was a certain expression on his face at the moment that brooked no nonsense.

"In telling you my shameful story, I must at the same time tell you something of our Scottish history. For without that knowledge you will not be understanding the events that brought Mary Queen of Scots to this castle on that tragic night in 1568.

"It was a time of bitter dissension in Scotland. Brother fought against brother. Father against son. The Clan MacSpurtle, long our hated enemy, came out for Mary. I, as the seventh Earl of Strathullen, was sorely tempted to do likewise, for I loved the young queen. Alas, my cowardice held me back as I feared what would happen to me should Mary's side lose.

"It was against this background of unbridled passion that I received word that Mary's husband, Lord Darnley, had been murdered. Her lover, the wild and impetuous Earl of Bothwell, was blamed, rightly or wrongly, for the foul deed. A group of scheming nobles, led by the queen's half-brother, seized the opportunity to have her thrown into Lochleven, a prison situated on an island not far from here. There, one dark night, a small band of her closest friends, led by Calum MacSpurtle, helped her escape. He was with her when she arrived at Strathullen Castle seeking refuge.

"I can see that scene as clearly today as I saw it that wild and stormy night. There was the Queen of Scotland, noble and beautiful, yet sorely fatigued from her imprisonment and her flight. There was Calum MacSpurtle, a great mountain of a man, arrogant and proud, the enemy of my people. There were Mary's small band of loyal followers, whose very lives would be in danger should they be caught. And there was I, Duncan MacDhu, the cowardly Earl of Strathullen.

"No one had seen them come, so dark was the night, so lashed with wind and rain. Mary asked, she did not plead, that her party be allowed sanctuary in the castle until such time as she could rally her forces and regain her crown. But I was weak and frightened, fearful of the fate that would befall me should it become known that I had har-

bored the queen. Despite all the pity I felt for the lass—for she was no more than that—I took her aside and told her she would have to be gone by morning. That I had no choice at all if I were to keep my lands here at Strathullen. I remember how she looked at me. Her eyes were dark and calm and there was no hatred in them. Only something, pity maybe, for this miserable creature who was the Earl of Strathullen. The next morning she was gone. Gone to England and the ungenerous cousin who was Queen Elizabeth and who would later have her head cut off. And it was all my fault, lad. All my fault."

Kenny said nothing. What was there he could possibly say? All he could feel at the moment was an aching compassion for the pathetic little figure before him. It was while he was sitting grief-stricken that he suddenly remembered something. Something that Mr. MacDhu had clearly forgotten to mention. "But you still have not told me how you became a ghost."

"Aye, that is so, for it is not easy to tell. Yet tell you I will." His face was gray with what might have been pain. "It was when the queen and the others were about to leave the next morning that Calum MacSpurtle burst into this room. Clearly my old enemy had just heard the news and his face was livid with rage. 'Damn you, MacDhu!' he cried. 'Damn you for a white-livered coward! You want this house and these grounds above everything else? Well, keep them! For no grave would want your miserable body. No kirkyard give decent sanctuary to your vile dust!' Then he pointed his finger at me, his eyes blazing. 'Until such a time as a MacSpurtle will regret the curse I now make, you are doomed to haunt these walls, these grounds, knowing no peace, no rest. Never!' The next moment he turned on his heel and was gone.

"And so it has been. It was only a few weeks

after the queen had left that I died. Perhaps of a broken heart. Perhaps of shame. Yet, true to the curse of my ancient enemy, my craven body could not rest in the little kirkyard of St. Fillan. So I am doomed to haunt these corridors forever. I would not give up Strathullen in life. I cannot escape it in death."

Kenny had never felt so miserable, so helpless. If only there were something he could say. Only there was nothing. Nothing at all.

Mr. MacDhu shook his head sorrowfully. "If there were only some way that this awful curse could be lifted from me, but alas, there is none. With the queen's forces defeated, the MacSpurtles of Glen Arley were ruthlessly outlawed and destroyed. And with no one left of that clan, there is no one who can undo the curse of Calum MacSpurtle." He looked down at his bloodless hands and sighed. The sigh seemed to come from the very depths of his being. "A coward."

And all at once the words, undammed, rushed with desperate haste from Kenny's lips, "You're not really a coward, Mr. MacDhu! You're not! Why, just telling me everything as you did proves you're not a coward! It took courage to do that. Besides, lots of brave men have been cowards at some time in their lives. Furthermore, a lot of people today think wars are stupid. Why, my dad says it often takes more guts not to fight than to fight!"

"True enough, lad, but such people have worthy motives. Their nobility uplifts them. They are at peace with themselves. But I have no such nobility. No such peace. I deserted what honor I had when I deserted my queen. And that is my story, my young American friend, and a sad story it is for certain. Now all I ask is that those—those toffee makers go away and leave me in peace."

Kenny looked glum. "I wish I could help you, but I can't. You see, it's all up to Mr. Budlong. It's his company."

"But my castle," snapped Mr. MacDhu.

"If only there were something we could do! Duggie—he's my friend—is real sharp, but he watches too many private eye shows. He's convinced you and Mrs. Wheerie are closer than Bonnie and Clyde and that you're up to no good. I'll have to think of some other way to help you."

"Nothing can help, lad. And now I must go, for the telling of my shameful story has wearied me. Should you want me at any time, look for me here in this room. So until we next meet, farewell!"

"But Mr. MacDhu—" Kenny began, before he

realized that the little figure in the kilt was slowly fading away before his eyes again. Now the feet with the buckled shoes were gone, then the legs, then the face. Kenny watched, mouth agape, as the feather on the Highland bonnet seemed to swim past him. The next moment it, too, was gone.

Only the picture over the mantelpiece remained. The picture of a little man in Highland costume who had died in 1568.

9

Flavors!" grumbled Mr. Spencer at the break-
fast table a week later. "I'm going crazy! Fraser's has had one flavor for a hundred years and
now Homer Budlong wants me to come up with a
dozen new ones overnight! Calls me up from Beverly Hills to find out why the delay. How am I supposed to know what's going to sell and what isn't?
I've got no market research people here in Auchterlony."

"What did they do before, Jim?" asked Mrs.
Spencer.

"Nothing, Nancy! All Fraser's ever had in that
area was one old man named Sandy Menzies. His
job was to sit at a bench and sample the toffee

each day. Just to be sure it was up to the standard set by old Andrew Fraser, the founder. When Sandy died twenty years ago, they didn't bother to fill the job."

Nancy Spencer smiled as she salted her boiled egg. "Come, Jim, it's not that bad. Didn't you say that your toffee sales have been booming lately?"

Jim Spencer grunted and buttered a hot roll. "But not enough to satisfy Homer Budlong! He claims I've got the ball in midfield now. It's still a long way before we score that touchdown."

Mrs. Spencer winked across the table at Kenny. "But don't forget the interference you've got when you carry the ball. Old Crazy-legs Hepplewaithe, no less!" She poured herself a cup of tea. "Anyway, I've been giving some thought to the flavor problem."

"You have?" For some reason Jim Spencer's face looked gloomier than before. "What do you know about flavors?"

"Nothing."

"So?"

"But I know Kenny."

"Kenny?" exclaimed Mr. Spencer.

"Kenny?" exclaimed Kenny.

"Kenny," reiterated Mrs. Spencer. "Look, Jim,

you have no one else, right? And you're not going to be able to put together a market research team in a place like Auchterlony for weeks."

Mr. Spencer's puzzled eyes traveled from his wife to his son. "But—"

"Look, Jim, who is the biggest market for toffee? Kids, right?"

"Yes, but—"

"And is Kenny a kid?"

"Sure, only—"

"Only nothing, Jim! And not just a kid, but a kid's kid! As average as they come. Not too smart, but not too dumb either. Not too pushy, yet not too shy. Never an outstanding jock at sports, yet a good, steady jayvee. Average height and weight for his age. And although *I* think he's something special, I'll have to admit that, as far as the public is concerned, he comes across as a typical, run-of-the-mill boy. So try your flavors on him!"

Jim Spencer looked bemused. "You know, you might just have something. A kid's kid. Why not? And all he has to do is sample the stupid flavors. He can't be any worse than old Sandy Menzies who was eighty-five when he died. If nothing else it will give us some breathing space until I can recruit a professional staff." He wheeled around to his son. "O.K., Kenny, you're hired. You're the official taster as of today. All you have to do is tell us when you think a particular flavor clicks."

Kenny nibbled thoughtfully on the corner of a thickly buttered oatcake. "Mm. What kind of money is in this thing, Dad?"

"None!" snapped his father. "If I start paying you I'm in violation of the British Child Labor Laws."

"You mean if you don't pay me, that makes it legal?" asked Kenny in an aggrieved voice.

"You're considered a non-salaried consultant." Mr. Spencer spread Dundee marmalade on his roll. He hesitated as though coming to a decision. "Of course you get the toffee for nothing."

Nancy Spencer laughed. "Let's face it, Kenny, when you get something like your father's Puritan Work Ethic and bring it over to a no-nonsense place like Scotland, a nice average kid like you just doesn't have a chance!"

To say the results were sensational would have been the understatement of the year. Ensconced in a plush office, Kenny spent the next weeks surrounded by heaps of toffee bars. When he had finished sampling one bar, he would rinse out his mouth before starting in on another. And no sooner did he give his official approval to a flavor than the public was clamoring for it. Jim Spencer had to admit he had never seen anything like it and promptly canceled his plans for a professional research staff.

Now and then Duggie came over to lend a hand, or a tooth, as he put it. "Nice set-up you've got yourself here, Kenny," he said on one such occasion. "I hear you're batting a thousand. Old Budlong must love you like a brother."

Kenny scowled. "Why shouldn't he? I don't cost him a dime. With guys like me on the payroll he's laughing all the way to the bank."

Duggie nodded but his thoughts seemed else-

where as he frowned off into space. "Haven't seen much of Mrs. Wheerie lately," he said casually.

"She's around."

Duggie's eyes hooded. "She's up to something. The last time I saw her she looked me right in the eye. Like she had nothing to hide." He lowered his voice. "The first rule in criminology is never to trust anybody who looks you right in the eye."

"Knock it off, Duggie. You see too many James Bond movies."

"Double-o seven?" The young Scot grunted. "Funny, he's the only shamus I don't like. Ever notice how the bad guy is always ugly or crippled? What's Bond got against—"

"That blasted Madison Avenue hokum! We don't need it over here!"

Kenny swung around in his chair at the sound of the furious voice. He hadn't heard his father's entry, possibly because of the thick carpeting on the floor. Jim Spencer's face was red as he glared at the cable in his hands. "What's up, Dad?" Kenny asked.

"Not my spirits!" his father snapped. His strong fingers crushed the cable into a ball. "They're going crazy out on the coast! Or at least Homer Budlong's going crazy. First he asks me to airship

114

him twelve dozen Forfar Bridies, baked by Mrs. Wheerie of course—"

"What?" gasped Kenny. "How can he pack away twelve dozen?"

Jim Spencer scowled. "How the devil do I know? But that's not the part that has me climbing the walls! It's the rest of his cable. First he tells me what a great job we're doing over here. Then he says we have to exploit our success with a gigantic public relations program. So I'm elected to organize something he calls Fraser's Highland Games! Right on the grounds of Strathullen Castle!"

"Fraser's Highland Games?" repeated Duggie, puzzled. "What has that got to do with selling toffee, Mr. Spencer?"

Jim Spencer gritted his teeth. "Not much, Duggie. It's the publicity angle he's after. Him and his hype tripe! I guess he figures it's a natural tie-in with his Highland milk gimmick." He laughed harshly.

"Gosh!" exclaimed Kenny. "And you say it's all gonna take place right here on the castle grounds?"

His father nodded glumly. "Tells me to get cracking on lining up bagpipe bands, Highland dancers, and something called caber tossers." He stared again at the message. "Caber tossers? You don't think he meant cable tossers? If he did, here's a cable I'd like to toss all the way back to Beverly Hills!" He closed his eyes and emitted a long soft sigh. "One thing for sure. Life was a lot less complicated when I was peddling Mrs. Kleinschmidt's Frozen Waffles!"

⚛ 10

Highland Games? Here on my grounds? Och, and you can't be serious, lad? Who would dare—"

"Mr. Budlong," cut in Kenny. "Homer M. Budlong." He hated to see the little ghost so upset, and he was beginning to regret his decision to tell him about the upcoming Games. Still, the earl was going to find out anyway. It was only fair that he know the reasons behind it.

"Budlong," muttered Mr. MacDhu. "Strange, I'm beginning to hate the man as much as I hated Calum MacSpurtle, the one who put the curse on me." He was silent for a long while as he restlessly paced his bedroom. "And when will all this start?"

"In three weeks. Duggie's father is making arrangements to get the bagpipe bands here. They're coming from as far away as Canada."

"No!" whispered Mr. MacDhu. His face was ashen. "I hate the pipes! All that wild skirling—"

"You hate the pipes?" Kenny exclaimed in shocked amazement. "But I thought all Scotsmen—"

"You will be forgetting, Kenny, that I am no the same as my countrymen. I am a coward. It was to the skirl of the pipes that my clansmen advanced to battle. Whenever I heard them in the old days I trembled and hid. They were like a chorus of shrill voices calling me to my duty." He swallowed hard. "And all I could do was hide."

Kenny looked at the floor. Anywhere other than at Mr. MacDhu's face.

"And what else is this Budlong planning, Kenny?"

"For the Games? Dad mentioned something about a caber-tossing contest. Duggie says it's a contest where you have to flip big poles through the air. Sounds kinda crazy."

"Caber tossing, eh?" An expression of interest flickered for a moment across the gentle face. "Well, well." He stared out the window, seemingly lost in thought. Suddenly he spun around and leaned forward. With an agility that astonished the boy, he whipped the *sgian-dubh* from his stocking.

The glistening point of the deadly weapon resting on his forefinger, Mr. MacDhu moved it in a series of gentle arabesques. Finally, to Kenny's amazement, the extended finger seemed to relax under the dagger point. The *sgian-dubh* was standing motionless in midair!

"You will observe, lad," said Mr. MacDhu with a dry smile, "that the laws of physics mean little in the spirit world. We are not subject to natural forces, as you may have noticed in my comings and goings." He seemed secretly amused as he returned the dagger to his stocking. "Anyway, no matter. Where have you been, lad? I have no seen you at all lately."

"I've been helping my father in the business," Kenny said importantly. "They're letting me pick

the flavors for the toffee. You might say I'm the guy who's really got the wheels spinning around Auchterlony. I mean, where would Howard Johnson be if he could only peddle vanilla?"

Mr. MacDhu nodded politely, a slightly puzzled cast to his face. "Howard Johnson? I'm afraid I've never met the man. Still, no matter. We have other things to reflect on. Like this Homer Budlong creature and his blasted Highland Games." He sighed. "I'm afraid, Kenny, I'm beginning to show my age. It's all too much for me." On what seemed an impulse he suddenly thrust his hand into the sporran of his kilt and took a small coin from the purse. "You are a good lad, I'd like you to have this bawbee for your patience in listening to an old man's daft ramblings. Buy yourself some sweets or cakes. There is no sense we should both be sad."

Kenny was on the point of protesting when he remembered Duggie telling him once that in the Highlands it is an insult to refuse any gift given with a good heart. He mumbled his thanks, put the coin in his pocket, and stared moodily out the window at the scene below. Preparations for Homer Budlong's Highland Games were well underway. Already a convoy of foul-smelling Diesel trucks, stacked with benches and camp chairs, were churning across the lawn. A group of workers had started to remove a stand of graceful birch trees, presumably for a parking lot. He turned away from the window, sick at heart.

"Don't worry—" he began, then stopped. Mr. MacDhu was gone! The boy stared around the room. Surely he couldn't have vanished so suddenly into thin air? Yet why not? Spirits were different from ordinary people. He suddenly remembered the little game Mr. MacDhu had played with the dagger. No doubt it had been too painful for him to see what was going on beyond his window. To watch the desecration of his beloved grounds. The grounds, shimmering with roses and honeysuckle whose fragrance had perfumed the soft Highland air since time began. And now it was all ending in a stench of Diesel fumes and choking dust.

Kenny felt the quick rush of pity deep within him. Poor, timid, frightened Mr. MacDhu! If only there was some way he might help him. Only there was nothing he, or anyone else, could do. Calum MacSpurtle, the chief of the Clan MacSpurtle, had done it all when he had uttered his terrible curse that fearful night in 1568.

Kenny's shoulders slumped. He took one final look at the portrait over the mantelpiece. Then he slowly made his way downstairs.

☀ *11*

"It's simply amazing, Kenny!" exclaimed Mr. Spencer a week later as the boy and his parents stood watching the workmen rushing to get everything in order for the opening day of the Highland Games. "I mean, the way you continue to pick the flavors that sell. It's uncanny!"

Kenny affected an air of studied nonchalance. "So I have a rare gift, Dad," he confessed with a shrug. "Of course it's harder when it's not hereditary. I mean, you and Mom don't have the knack. You both could hardly tell the difference between Fraser's toffee and Mrs. Kleinschmidt's frozen waffles."

"Knock it off, Kenny Spencer," his mother returned. "So you're an average kid, tuned in to what the average kid likes. Big deal."

"Whatever it is, it's certainly got Homer Budlong excited," said Mr. Spencer. "By the way, I made it a point to stress that everything was Kenny's doing. H.M. was really impressed."

"That makes two of us," Kenny said. He grinned at his mother.

"He also asked me to airship him another supply of Mrs. Wheerie's Forfar Bridies. Where on earth does he put them all?" Jim Spencer shook his head in unbelief.

"He's certainly flipped over them, that's for sure," said Mrs. Spencer. "Is he coming over for the Games?"

"Is he? This is his baby! A team of those big Clydesdale horses couldn't keep him away." Jim Spencer let his eyes drift with satisfaction over the activities on the field where they were standing. "You can't say things haven't been happening around here, and it's all thanks to Ian Cameron. Man, am I ever glad to have him around! I couldn't organize a Sunday School picnic, far less a specialized shindig like this. I mean, how could I go about lining up sword dancers, caber tossers, and a bunch of people who read Gaelic poetry all day? Ian has even arranged to have a mini Sheep

Dog Trials and the shepherds will be bringing along their little collies from miles around. Yep, despite what I thought earlier, it's going to be quite a day, both for Fraser's Creamy Toffee and our leader, Homer M. Budlong."

Kenny said nothing, his thoughts suddenly elsewhere. Poor Mr. MacDhu! All he ever wanted was peace and quiet. Well, from the looks of things, it was precious little of either he would be getting from here on in.

"Something wrong, Kenny? You seem awfully quiet." It was his mother who asked the question.

"Uh? Oh nothing, Mom. I was just watching them put up that purple-colored pavilion in front of the grandstand. Gold fringe and tassels. Don't tell me the royal family is coming?"

His father grinned. "Royal family? In a way. Not the British one. The American one. Homer M. Budlong himself. That's for his exclusive use, as the guest of honor. Hepplewaithe arranged it from California." He glanced at his son. "Where are you off to, Kenny?"

"Going to see Duggie. Remember you gave me the day off, Dad? What was that the man said? 'All work and no pay—' "

"Play, not pay." His father grunted. "You make

me feel like Scrooge. O.K., run along, then. See you later."

Duggie wasn't home when Kenny got there, but Duggie's mother suggested he might be found near an old stone cairn at the edge of Glen Arley where he often went. Kenny had no difficulty in finding the mound of weathered stones that no doubt marked some bloody struggle in days gone by. He was relieved when he drew nearer to find Duggie, his back propped against the monument, an Agatha Christie paperback in his hands. Duggie's face lit up when he recognized his American friend.

"Kenny! What brings you here? I thought you'd be molar deep in new toffee flavors."

Kenny eased himself down alongside the cairn. "Dad gave me the day off. Or rather my taste buds." He nibbled on a stem of satin-smooth purple heather. "I was just watching them getting ready for the Games. Did you know Budlong's gonna have his own pavilion?" He laughed mirthlessly and stared with disinterest as a whaup fluttered up from the distant peat hags, then swept in great circles over the solitary glen.

Duggie eyed him quizzically. "Something's bothering you, friend. Anything wrong?"

Kenny shrugged. "Nothing, I guess. Just don't like what they're doing to the grounds around the castle. What the world doesn't need right now is another crummy parking lot."

"Well," murmured Duggie, his blue eyes shrewd. "So something *is* on your mind. Not that little dude who's been hiding out at Strathullen?"

Kenny nodded. "But he's not what you think he is. There's nothing like Mr. MacDhu in any of these books you read." He hesitated, regrouping his thoughts. "Did you ever hear of anyone called Calum MacSpurtle? Away back in your history?"

"Calum MacSpurtle?" Duggie knitted his brows and put away his paperback. "Yeah, I've heard of him. He was the last chief of the Clan MacSpurtle before he was outlawed. There are no more Mac-Spurtles around Glen Arley. Not anywhere, I guess. Not since the time of Mary Queen of Scots."

Kenny could feel the slow build-up of excitement deep inside him. "Do you know if he was with her the night she came to Strathullen Castle? Think hard."

Duggie dug his fingers into his red hair. "Hey, man, what am I? Some kind of weird whiz kid? I can tell you that the MacSpurtles were on the queen's side, anyway. In fact, Calum MacSpurtle was one of her chief supporters. I understand he helped her escape from Lochleven, so it is probable that he was with her when she came to Strathullen Castle that night. It was shortly afterward, with Mary defeated, that the Clan MacSpurtle was outlawed for the part it had played in the uprising." He looked curiously at the American. "What brings all this up?"

"Nothing," whispered Kenny, his eyes glistening. So the story fitted! There *had* been a Calum MacSpurtle and almost certainly he had arrived with the queen that night! And the clan *had* been outlawed just as Mr. MacDhu had said! On an impulse Kenny dug his hand into his pocket and passed a small coin to his friend. "Did you ever see anything like this?"

Duggie's eyes narrowed in concentration. "Say, this is old! Seems to me I remember reading about a small coin like this one. A bawbee, they called it. But that was ages ago."

"Read what's inscribed on the other side, Duggie."

The redhead reversed the bawbee and his jaw dropped. "MARIA DEI GRA R. SCOTOR." His voice was hushed, almost a whisper. "And see here, Kenny? A crowned thistlehead and a fleurde-lis. Mary was brought up in France." He looked stunned as he returned the coin. "Where on earth did you find it?"

Kenny said quietly, "Mr. McDhu gave it to me."

"Mr. MacDhu? But that's crazy, Kenny! Where would a tinker get a rare coin like this? And why should he give it away?" Duggie sighed and smiled ruefully. "O.K., O.K. Me and my screwball deductions. I guess I do watch too many cops-and-robbers shows. So this little guy in the castle can't be a tinker, whatever else he is." He made himself more comfortable against the cairn. "Kenny, do me a favor. Tell me everything this little dude told you. Everything. And this time I promise not to act like a pint-size Columbo with a heather accent."

"O.K." Hesitantly at first, then with growing confidence as he went along, Kenny related everything that Mr. MacDhu had told him. Of the things that had taken place that grim night when Mary and her little band of followers arrived at the castle, seeking sanctuary. Of the earl's fear of getting involved and losing his estates and possibly his life. Of the awful curse that Calum MacSpurtle had hurled at him. There was a long pause after Kenny finished before Duggie spoke. His face was somber. So was his voice.

"And now, Kenny, I will tell you a story. A stranger story. It was in all our local newspapers at the time. It never made much sense to me. I think it does now.

"Three years ago they had to lay new drainage pipes in Auchterlony. In the course of the job they had to move some of the bodies buried in the old kirkyard of St. Fillan. Everything went fine until they opened the grave of the seventh Earl of Strathullen."

Kenny looked up when his friend fell silent. "And?"

"There was nothing in the coffin. No bones. No dust. Nothing!"

✺ 12

Auchterlony was alive with flags the great day of the Fraser Highland Games. Kenny had never seen so many banners. The British Union Jack. The blue and white St. Andrew's Cross. The ancient Lion Rampant of Scotland. They whipped from the freshly painted white poles. They garlanded lampposts. They hung from windows. They were draped across High Street. As they snapped in the wind, Kenny found himself caught up in the excitement all around him while the buses poured through the village from the surrounding countryside.

The newly erected stands beyond the castle were almost completely filled by the time Kenny and

Duggie got there. The boys had been delayed in getting inside because Mr. Cameron had asked Duggie to hand out souvenir toffee pennants at the gates. Although impatient to see what was going on, Kenny had insisted on helping his friend. He was vastly relieved when Duggie abruptly brought the giveaway to a close by presenting the last two boxes of pennants to a group of urchins from the village. The two boys just had time to squeeze into their seats before Duggie spotted the helicopter flying in from the direction of Strathullen Castle. It circled the grounds twice before coming to rest in the middle of the field. The whirling rotors finally ceased spinning and, in a moment, the door of the cabin swung open.

In all his life, Kenny would never forget the apparition that greeted his eyes as Homer Budlong emerged. From the ample waist of UGH's president hung a kilt of a strident tartan, and oversized silver buttons studded his green velvet jacket. Covering his bald head was a wide-brimmed Western hat. On his feet were a pair of soft leather cowboy boots. And on his face was a grin that spread from ear to ear as he waved to the packed stands.

"No!" gasped Kenny. "I don't believe it! Kilts

and cowboy boots! And a ten-gallon hat to top it off!"

Duggie grinned. "But the crowd loves it. Just listen to the cheers! It's the perfect public relations gimmick. The union of California and old Scotland. Fraser's Toffee is really in the big leagues now!"

"You can say that again," said Kenny, an edge of grimness to his voice, "only don't bother."

The Games started with the traditional marchpast of the assembled bands. Gallant in their High-

land costumes, their sporrans swinging, their white spats flashing, the marchers strutted in front of the reviewing stand while the air trembled with the wild skirl of the beribboned pipes. Event followed event after that, sword dancing and stone putting and sheepherding, until finally came an announcement that the caber tossers should check in and take up their positions on the field.

The caber tossers. Kenny leaned forward on his bench. He had been curious about the sport since his father had first mentioned it. He watched intently as an enormous bear of a kilted man gripped a tree trunk that must have been all of seventeen feet. His biceps writhing under the strain, he raised it off the ground. Poising it with his jaw and shoulder, the huge pole teetering above him, he scrambled forward for a distance of about eight feet. Balancing himself and stamping his two heels firmly into the turf, he raised the caber with the tips of his fingers until the base was almost level with his neck. The muscles on his legs and arms corded as the great pole made a complete somersault and crashed to the earth.

"Gosh!" whispered Kenny, round eyed with awe and admiration. "Did you see what that guy just did, Duggie? He tossed that telegraph pole like it was some kind of matchstick!"

Duggie nodded. "Notice how the caber landed on one end, then fell forward on a direct line from where it was released? That's called the 'twelve o'clock mark,' and when you can do that, you're tops. Incidentally, you'll notice the build on those guys. You've got to be Tarzan Senior just to raise the caber off the ground."

Kenny grinned. "I couldn't get one of those things off the ground with a jack." He stared at the ten contestants. They were all of gargantuan build, with thick brawny shoulders that swelled to powerful biceps and forearms. Despite their obvious strength, however, several of them had difficulty in achieving the rotary motion needed to flip the caber over. The first contestant, a sandy-haired giant, was judged the winner on the basis of a near perfect toss that brought the crowd to its feet.

The contest over, Homer Budlong, resplendent in kilt and ten-gallon hat, emerged from his pavilion to present the trophies to the winners. All eyes were riveted on the scene below when Kenny, idly turning his head for a moment, chanced to catch a glimpse of a small kilted figure furtively making its way from under the stands. Suddenly, with a swiftness that brought a cry of astonishment to Kenny's lips, the intruder was on the field and had seized a caber. Only then did the crowd become aware of his presence. A roar went up as the small figure, bent under the massive pole, made its way toward the pavilion. Homer Budlong, presiding over his trophy table, looked up with annoyance when he heard the noise. The cigar popped out of his mouth when he realized what was happening.

"It's Mr. MacDhu!" cried Kenny.

"No!" gasped Duggie. "You're sure?"

"I'd know him anywhere! And that kilt he's wearing! Dark green and blue squares and thin

white stripes. I've never seen a tartan like it."

"But Kenny! Look at the size of him! How can he even lift that thing?"

Kenny, remembering the incident with the dagger, was fairly certain he knew the secret but thought it better to keep silent. Some things like natural and unnatural law you can't hope to explain. Even to one's best friend.

Homer Budlong's initial astonishment had now given way to anger. Clearly he did not relish the idea of sharing the spotlight with this half-pint country bumpkin. Suspicious by nature, the thought must also have occurred to him that the whole thing was some kind of hoax. The caber itself was almost surely made of plastic or some fiberboard substance. His heavy jowls quivering with indignation, he advanced toward the intruder. With his imposing appearance and air of authority, he looked like a chief executive who had just caught the office boy in the act of pilfering the coffee money.

"I'll take that, my man," he snapped, indicating the caber. "Now!"

The small intruder glanced up. "You're sure you want it?" he inquired softly. His shoulders moved in what might have been a shrug. "Then take it!" The next moment the pole was soaring lazily through the air, almost as though it were made of straw.

His suspicions of the caber verified by its airborne properties, Homer Budlong permitted a grim smile of satisfaction to flit across his face. He had just thrust out his hands to cradle the object when the full weight and force of the seventeen-foot pole hit him. With a howl loud enough to awaken the dead in the nearby churchyard of St. Fillan, the president of United Groceries Holdings crashed to the ground.

Possibly it was the ten gallon hat that saved him from a serious head injury. Possibly it was his own thick skull and muscular body. Wherever his good fortune lay, he escaped with only a collection of bruises, bumps, and contusions that transformed his beefy face into an artist's palette of assorted colors. Satisfied that there were no broken bones, Jim Spencer and Ian Cameron finally got their boss to his feet.

It took Homer Budlong a full ten minutes to collect his breath, straighten his kilt, and brush the dust from his green velvet jacket. One eye almost completely closed, he glowered around him with the other. "Where is he?" he muttered. "That little creep who hit me? I'll—I'll kill him!"

Jim Spencer frowned. "That's odd. He was here just a few moments ago. I guess with all the excitement he disappeared into the crowd."

Ian Cameron's face was thoughtful. "What I can't understand is how someone his size could possibly have tossed that caber the way he did. It was more than three times as big as he was."

"If I ever get my hands on him—!" snarled Budlong. He dabbed a silk handkerchief against his bruised mouth. "Where did the little nut come from, anyway? All of a sudden, there he was on the field with that crazy telegraph pole." He moaned softly as he massaged his ribs.

There was a puzzled expression on Jim Spencer's face. "I don't know why, Homer, but it seems to me he came from the direction of the castle. That side of the field, anyway. Odd-looking little fellow. Funny, he seemed almost frightened. As though he were doing something he didn't like to do, but had to do."

"Never saw him around Auchterlony before," said Ian Cameron decisively. "I know everyone in these parts. And that little pasty face I wouldn't forget too readily."

Homer Budlong grunted. "I suppose the photographers had a field day when I was flat on my back under that big pole?"

Jim Spencer nodded. "I'm afraid so, Homer. There's sure to be lots of publicity. Still, that was the idea." He winked at Ian Cameron.

"It wasn't the idea to have me murdered by some Highland nut!" snapped Budlong. He smoothed his battered hat before easing it down gently on his bruised head. "Well, I'd better be on my way. Got a big meeting tomorrow in Paris. The helicopter will get me to the airport."

"Sorry you've got to go, Homer," said Jim Spencer as they shook hands by the cabin of the helicopter. "You're sure you're all right now?"

Budlong did not answer him, his thoughts apparently elsewhere. There was a frown on his face as he stared at the parapets of Strathullen Castle and the wine-red hills beyond Glen Arley. "Weird sort of place," he muttered. "The mist and the moor and the castle. I feel almost as though I had seen it before. A long time ago."

Jim Spencer exchanged a startled glance with Ian Cameron. "You're sure I shouldn't get a doctor, Homer? That hit on the head—"

"Forget it, Jim! Keep on selling. I'll be in touch." Homer Budlong clambered painfully into the cabin and the rotors started to spin. The next moment he was soaring high over the field.

Jim Spencer stared thoughtfully after the aircraft as it climbed ever higher in the sky. "I wonder what he meant, Ian. About having been here before, a long time ago."

Ian Cameron shrugged. "The hit on the head. It just had to be that."

The other nodded. "I suppose you're right." But the thoughtful expression was still on Jim Spencer's face when the helicopter vanished behind the hills.

✹ 13

Although Kenny was almost beside himself in his eagerness to talk over the day's events with Mr. MacDhu, it was impossible for him to slip away without being noticed. The next several days were filled with chores following the dismantling of the stands and in helping his father handle the publicity that had resulted from the Games. Accordingly it was nearly a week before Kenny was able to sneak away after lunch to the meeting room upstairs. He was bitterly disappointed to find it empty when he entered.

"Are you there?" he whispered. "It's me, Kenny Spencer."

There was no answer. "Mr. MacDhu?" He hesitated when again there was no reply. "It was you, wasn't it, who tossed that caber at Mr. Budlong? Everyone's talking about it and it's in all the papers and on television. You've made Fraser's the best-known toffee in the whole wide world!"

Kenny waited in the stillness. It was strange. The little ghost had always been there before. Yet clearly he wasn't there now. Or if he was, he chose to remain invisible. Yet why should he want to do that? Kenny waited for a few more moments, then made his way slowly downstairs, uneasy for a reason he could not have explained.

When he got to the kitchen Mrs. Wheerie was there, his mother having gone lawn bowling with Mrs. Cameron and some of the other women as they always did on Saturdays. The housekeeper looked up from her paste rolling when he entered.

"So it's yourself, lad? Ye will be finding it a bit quiet I'm thinking, now that the Games are gone."

He nodded. "Yeah." He suddenly realized that he hadn't seen Mrs. Wheerie during the Games. "Were you there?"

"A lot o' sinful nonsense! Grown men flinging hammers and tugging at wee bits o' rope! Aye, and that dreadful business o' striking poor Mr. Budlong! No, ye won't see me at such goings-on."

Kenny's eyes flickered quick interest. "If you weren't at the Games, Mrs. Wheerie, how did you know what happened to Mr. Budlong?"

"It's all over Auchterlony, is it no?" She did not look at the boy.

He decided to change the subject. "What are you making there, Mrs. Wheerie?"

"Forfar Bridies, no less." A small smile tugged at her stern mouth.

"Again?" He stared. "For California?"

She hesitated. "Not for California. For Mr. Budlong. Did you know he came here to the castle before the Games? Just to tell me how much he liked them? Wasn't that decent o' the man, though?"

Kenny nodded but said nothing. He noticed idly that Mrs. Wheerie was wearing her hair differently and that her dress, though still black, seemed somehow less somber. No doubt the mourning period for her last husband was nearly over. The boy shrugged. It was none of his business. "See you later, Mrs. Wheerie. Would you mind telling Mom I went over to Duggie's? Thanks."

His friend was working in the small vegetable garden behind his cottage when Kenny got there.

His face was red with exertion and frustration as he jabbed his pitchfork into the flinty soil. His expression changed to relief when he recognized his caller.

"Saved!" Duggie exclaimed as he tossed his pitchfork aside. "The only things that flourish in this rock pile are blisters and backaches!" He led the way into the kitchen. "What's up, Kenny?

Something's on your mind. I can read you like a book." He grinned as he poured two tall glasses of lemonade. "Better, considering the way I read some books."

"It's Mr. MacDhu. I can't find him anywhere."

Duggie frowned. "Maybe he took a walk. It's a big castle."

Kenny shook his head.

"Then maybe he's still recovering from the Games." He hesitated. "You're still sure he was the dude who almost scalped Homer?"

"Positive. You know, Duggie, I'm worried about him. He must have been awfully confused and upset to leave the castle and take on Mr. Budlong." He bit his lip. "You don't think he might do something—well—desperate?"

Duggie lifted an eyebrow. "You say he's been dead for four hundred years. How more desperate can you get?"

"Yeah." Kenny let his thoughts drift aimlessly. "Maybe I should speak to Dad. No, forget that. He'd never believe me. Besides, he's got enough on his mind these days with the sales skyrocketing as they have." He took a sip of his lemonade.

"I heard today they may have to move some of the production from Auchterlony to the castle.

That means they will be making toffee right in Strathullen."

"No!" gasped Kenny. "In the castle? But the noise, Duggie! Assembly lines and machinery. . . ." His voice trailed into silence.

Duggie must have guessed at the words unspoken. "As I said before, it's a big castle. I'm sure he'll be able to find someplace where he can get away from it all."

"Sure," returned Kenny bitterly. "Like maybe one of the dungeons."

Duggie shook his head dejectedly as he followed his friend to the door. "Look, Kenny, I know it's not fair, but what is these days? I'm sure everything's going to work out all right. In the meantime I'll try to think of something."

Kenny was surprised to find his father waiting for him when he got home, sitting in the library with a faraway look in his eyes. "You usually work on Saturday, Dad. Anything wrong?"

"Oh, there you are, Kenny. No, nothing wrong. Just Homer Budlong. He's going to drive me crazy. Just phoned me to confirm we have to expand our production to take care of all the orders that have been pouring in since the Highland Games. That means we will have to move in some machinery and start making toffee right here in the castle." He paused. "But I expected that. What I didn't expect was the bombshell that followed."

"Bombshell?"

"That's what it amounts to. He ordered me to drop all the flavors we've been making. Wants me now to standardize on one. *The* Fraser Creamy Toffee bar. Dump everything we've developed. Just like that." He closed his eyes and let his breath out in a long, soft sigh.

"What?" cried Kenny, his voice sharp with alarm and amazement. "After all our work? He's got to be kidding, Dad!"

"Oh, he knows what he's doing all right. It's a matter of profits, the well-known bottom line. You see, with the tremendous publicity we've been getting from the Games, we're no longer the modest little company we were. So Homer Budlong claims he's got to change his game plan." He scowled. "Why do all those big business hotshots think they have to talk like football coaches?"

"I still don't get it, Dad. Why the switch?"

"A matter of costs. You see, if you have a big product line, you have big costs. Every flavor has to be produced, packaged, and inventoried separately. You can tie up a lot of cash in the pipelines. And with the cost of money today, you could wind up in the red ink area. No, Homer Budlong knows what he's doing. Still, the whole thing comes as rather a shock."

"So, no more flavors. That means I'm unemployed again. Oh, well, my take-home pay wasn't so hot anyway." He grinned.

"Don't be too impatient, son. Before you start clearing out your desk we have to come up with a distinctively new flavor that will identify us in the future."

Kenny looked at him uneasily. "Who's this 'we'?"

"Actually, I should have said 'you.' Homer Budlong's orders. With a track record like yours, he said you were a natural for the job. He wants you and you alone to do the picking."

"Thanks," said Kenny glumly. "But suppose I strike out, Dad? Suppose this one new flavor bombs?"

Jim Spencer put his arm around his son. "It won't bomb, Kenny. You seem to have an instinctive feel for what pleases kids—and it's kids who buy toffee." He slipped his papers into a folder. "And now if you'll excuse me, I'll get back to work. We've got to figure how to set up the assembly line for the new production."

Leaving his father in the library, Kenny made his way slowly into the deserted great hall. The silence seemed to hang in the air like the faded banners suspended from the beamed ceiling. With the office workers home for the day, the stillness seemed a palpable thing, pressing in upon him from every side. Then suddenly, as though it was coming from another world, as well it might, he heard it. A thin, faint sound as though someone, a child perhaps, was sobbing. Then as quickly as it had come it was gone.

And the stillness in Strathullen Castle was as massive as before. And nothing stirred. And nothing moved.

⚛ *14*

It was not until four days later that Kenny met Mr. MacDhu, and met him where normally he would never have dreamed of looking. In a small grove at the end of a sunken garden just beyond the castle. Strolling aimlessly, relieved to be away from the noise and confusion of the great hall, Kenny simply had followed his feet to this most lonely and secluded of spots. It was the ancient sundial in the center of the grove that first caught his eye; then he realized that someone was sitting on a stone bench a few feet away.

"Mr. MacDhu!" he cried as he recognized the stoop-shouldered little figure with the bowed head. "What are you doing here?"

"Eh? Ah, it's yourself, Kenny?" The little ghost

sighed. "As to why I am here, it is simply enough answered. There is no place at all, at all, for me in my own castle. From morning until night the noise never seems to stop. And all those big black machines going up and down. Up and down." He sighed again.

"Dad says they used to do it all by hand. Now machines do it." Kenny looked away, embarrassed by the stricken look on his friend's face. "Mr. Budlong says you can't fight progress."

"So that's what they call it? I was wondering." Mr. MacDhu laughed without mirth. "Anyway, Kenny, I come here most days and just sit and think. Mostly I think why I didn't kill that Budlong creature when I had the chance."

"So it *was* you, Mr. MacDhu! I was sure of it!"

The small ghost stared off into space. Almost as though he hadn't heard the boy. "His face," he whispered. "It keeps coming back to me. Heavy and coarse. The jutting chin and the big beak of a nose. Could I have seen that face before? But where?" He sighed again. "Ah, well, no matter. I overheard you on Saturday, talking with your father. You can imagine how shocked I was to find out my castle was to become a toffee factory. I tried not to cry, but sometimes—" He gulped and bowed his head.

"Then that was you I heard—" Kenny began,

then bit the words back in his mouth. Some things are best not said.

"The castle of the Earls of Strathullen, a toffee factory," said Mr. MacDhu dolefully. He wrung his pale hands.

"If only I could help," Kenny said miserably.

"No one can help! No one—" The ghost stopped, apparently arrested by some vagrant thought. His brows grooved in a frown. "Perhaps you can, lad, come to think of it. That business that I overheard about the new flavor—"

"Yes?" prodded the boy when he did not continue.

"What would happen, now, if you picked the wrong one?"

Kenny shrugged. "So far I've been pretty good. Mr. Budlong thinks I can pick this one too."

Mr. MacDhu hesitated. "But suppose you *deliberately* picked the wrong one." He looked uncomfortable.

"If I picked a real dog? I guess it would be curtains for Fraser's Creamy Toffee. With only one bar on the market, the competition would murder us."

"And then?"

"Well, then I suppose we'd be out of the toffee business."

"And out of Strathullen Castle, too," added Mr.

MacDhu softly. For a moment, small lights gleamed deep in his eyes; then he suddenly stiffened. "No, lad! Never could I ask you to do such a thing! And it was cowardly of me to have given thought to it. You will forget the words I just spoke. Forget them entirely!"

"Sure," said Kenny agreeably, but he did not forget them. They kept tossing and turning in his mind long after he had left the little ghost. Suppose—just suppose—he did deliberately pick a flavor that would spell disaster for Fraser's? Would the company, would Homer Budlong, go along with it? But of course they would, based on everything his father had told him. They trusted him. They were depending on him. Should he choose to hurt them in any way, he would be more than an ingrate. He would be a traitor. He winced at the thought.

And of course there was his father. He was in charge of the plant. It was his responsibility to make the operation a financially successful one. If he did an outstanding job, there was no saying how high he might not go in the big conglomerate. But if what Mr. MacDhu had suggested took place, it almost surely would spell the end for any hopes his father might have of future advancement.

Kenny sighed. He was crazy even to think of it.

Yet what other hope did Mr. MacDhu have of regaining the peace and quiet he had always known in the castle? Nobody seemed to care about him. For that matter, nobody seemed to want to believe that he even existed. And if he, Kenny, didn't help, who else would? For that matter, who else could? Only Kenny had it in his power to help the ghost of Strathullen Castle. Only he.

The longer he pondered the matter, the more convinced he became that his first step should be to talk the whole thing over with Duggie.

The redheaded youngster listened with rapt attention when Kenny called at his cottage that afternoon. Not once did he interrupt his visitor, preferring to keep his thoughts to himself until Kenny finished.

"So what do you think, Duggie?" Kenny impatiently demanded after a few moments of silence.

The young Scot frowned. "Frankly, I think the whole thing is slightly nuts! I mean, if a billion-dollar outfit like UGH has to depend on a fourteen-year-old kid for its market research, then it deserves anything that happens to it."

"But they're counting on me, Duggie!"

"Yeah? How much are they paying you?"

"Nothing."

"So they should expect nothing. What do you owe Homer Budlong anyway, except maybe a couple of cavities for all that toffee you've been chewing?"

"But it's not just Homer Budlong. It's Fraser's!"

"Look, Kenny, Fraser's has been around for a hundred years. No matter what you do, chances are it will be around for another hundred years. Maybe it won't be a big global operation, but some guy here in Auchterlony will still be wrapping little pieces of colored papers around little pieces of colored candy. And they'll still call it Fraser's Creamy Toffee. So my advice is this. If you believe you can help this Mr. MacDhu, then go ahead and help him. And remember, you're not doing it for yourself. You're doing it for somebody else."

Kenny looked doubtful. "You mean I ought to feel noble about it?"

Duggie grimaced. "It's this way, Kenny. An awful lot of people today don't care for big multinational companies like UGH that go around the world gobbling up little companies as if they were so many pizzas or hot dogs. The little fellow doesn't have a chance any more. I'm not saying *you* have to figure it that way, but a lot of other people do."

Kenny took his time making his way back to the castle. There were a lot of things to turn over in his mind and none of them seemed to make too much sense. Could he possibly get away with it?

And what about the morality of it all? Duggie hadn't mentioned that aspect of it. What they had been discussing was the possible destruction of a company and its good name. And for what? So that a timid little ghost who had expired four hundred years ago might be left in peace. Kenny sighed.

He couldn't do it. Not to his own father.

"This is the one I pick," Kenny said.

"*This* is the one you pick, Kenny?" Jim Spencer frowned as he took the bar from his son and sniffed it. "Ugh!" he exlaimed as his nose wrinkled in disgust. "It smells like cod liver oil!"

"This is it, Dad! Kids won't smell it, they'll chew it." Kenny couldn't believe the words he had just said. He tried to avoid looking at Duggie who was sitting poker faced on the other side of the desk.

Mr. Spencer grunted and darted a quick look at Duggie's father as he studied the candy bar. "What do you think, Ian?"

Mr. Cameron made a wry face, then shrugged. "You're both right. Kids will decide if they like it when they chew it. And yes, it does smell like cod liver oil. You'll remember though, Jim, that Homer told us to try anything, particularly if it has vitamins in it. He claims there's a big market of health food nuts we haven't tapped yet. As to the smell, I'm sure our chemists can touch it up so you won't be aware of it too much." He turned to Kenny. "You really think this is the one we should go ahead with?"

Kenny nodded. He turned his head, ashamed to look Mr. Cameron in the face. He wanted to shout, "No, no, not that one," but instead the words, "You have to get used to it, sir," came tumbling out.

"Like limburger cheese," Duggie suggested, too solemnly.

"May I remind you, Duggie," snapped his father, "that we are not selling limburger cheese? We're selling toffee. Or trying to."

Jim Spencer smiled. "Cheer up, Ian. I'm sure it isn't that bad. And just think. Remember that deceptive differential gimmick that Homer was talking about? Well, now we've got ourselves a natural. We'll be the only company in the toffee business featuring cod liver oil!" He laughed sourly. "O.K., Ian, let's go. You and I have a lot to do before our breakthrough product hits the market." He sighed heavily as he moodily regarded the new toffee bar. "I just hope Homer Budlong knew what he was doing when he left all this up to Kenny Spencer!"

It's a disaster!" It was four weeks later that Jim Spencer burst into the kitchen, a sheaf of sales reports clenched in his fist. His face was grim as he accepted the cup of tea that Mrs. Wheerie handed him. "The first market reports on the new toffee bar are in. And they couldn't be more ghastly. We're getting cancellations from all our dealers. What a mess!"

"Oh, Jim!" exclaimed Nancy Spencer. She put her arm around his shoulders. "I'm so sorry! Isn't there anything you can do?"

Her husband shook his head gloomily. "Nothing. Of course we'll take it off the market. Still, the damage has been done. I've already cabled the bad news to Homer Budlong. If I know him, he'll be over on the next plane. Now all we can do is just sit nice and cozy in our castle and wait for the roof to fall in. Oh, well, we can't say it wasn't fun while it lasted."

"But it wasn't your fault, Jim! It was Mr. Budlong's. You were simply following his orders. If anybody is to blame, he is!"

"No," said Kenny in a voice that was half a whisper. He had never felt so miserable as he did at that moment. He had done a lot of soul searching over the last four weeks. Only now was he beginning to realize the enormity of the thing he had done. He stared straight ahead, his eyes glazed with pain, afraid to look at his parents. "It wasn't Mr. Budlong's fault. None of it. It was mine. All of it."

His father patted him roughly on the back. "Don't take it like that, Son. We had no business expecting you to undertake the crazy job we gave you. A fourteen-year-old kid doing the work of a highly specialized research team! I should have spoken up and told Homer Budlong he was out of his mind. But I didn't. I guess, deep down, I was secretly proud of you." He thrust his pipe between his teeth. "As for you, Kenny, you did your best. Forget it."

"But that's just it!" the boy exclaimed miserably. "I didn't do my best. I did my worst! Just like I planned to! But I didn't want to!" He could feel the stinging behind his eyes where the tears were. He knew his parents were staring at him. Even Mrs. Wheerie was regarding him oddly, her dark eyes probing and thoughtful.

Mr. Spencer took his pipe from his mouth. "What do you mean, Son?"

Kenny swallowed the lump in his throat. "Just that I knew I was picking the real dog! I knew what might happen to the company. And I did it anyway." His cheeks felt as though they were on fire. There was no sound in the kitchen.

"Why?" It was his mother who finally broke the silence. There was concern in her eyes, in her voice. "Why would you do a thing like that, Kenny?"

He ran his tongue over his dry lips. "I couldn't help it! I didn't do it for myself, Mom. I did it for Mr. MacDhu."

His father's eyes were cold as gunmetal. "And just who is Mr. MacDhu?"

Kenny hesitated. "I know it's not going to be easy for you to believe this, Dad, but Mr. MacDhu is the seventh Earl of Strathullen."

"Indeed?" An angry flush suffused Jim Spencer's face. "Is this some kind of sick joke? The seventh Earl of Strathullen died ages ago!"

"I know, Dad." Kenny swallowed hard. "Well, actually it's not the seventh Earl of Strathullen—"

"No?"

"It's his ghost."

"His ghost?" repeated his father. Anger put hard knots in his jaw as he regarded his son.

Kenny shook his head wearily. "I knew you would never believe me, Dad. That's why I never told you before. Only Duggie knows. You see, Mr. MacDhu is going out of his mind with everything that's been happening around here. I mean, for four hundred years he's had the castle all to himself, and now he's got to share it with a lot of toffee machines. And on top of everything else, for some reason he can't stand Mr. Budlong."

Mr. Spencer glanced over his shoulder. "So he lives with us here in the castle?" His voice sounded grim.

Kenny nodded. "Most of the time. You see, his grave is cursed so he can't rest there. That's in the little churchyard of St. Fillan. You can't miss his grave because there's no grass on it—"

"Stop it, Kenny!" snapped his father, his eyes blazing. "I've had enough of this drivel! You've been fantasizing ever since we got here. Do you realize what you've done? If what you said a moment ago is true, you've almost single-handedly wrecked a fine old company. And for what? Some cock-and-bull business about—"

"A cable for yourself, sir." It was Mrs. Wheerie, bearing an envelope on a tray.

"Thanks." Jim Spencer took the message, tore it open and read it silently. His strong fingers crumped it into a ball.

Mrs. Spencer looked at him quickly. "Bad news, Jim?"

"Homer Budlong got my cable and is flying over. Just as I feared. Meanwhile, as of today, I'm relieved of all my responsibilities with Fraser's Creamy Toffee."

"Oh!" cried Nancy Spencer in a shocked voice.

Kenny said nothing. His throat was too full for the words to squeeze through. Anyway, what was there to say?

His father had been fired from his job. And it was all his fault.

16

So that's it, Homer," Jim Spencer concluded as he swept his papers back into his briefcase. "You asked for a full report. You just got one." He hesitated and looked at his former boss. "I must confess I was surprised that you wanted to discuss this matter privately over the lunch table. The sales figures could hardly have helped your indigestion."

"Eh? Don't worry about it, Jim. These things happen in business. Besides, I was the one who insisted that Kenny pick the new Fraser toffee bar." Mr. Budlong seemed distraught, his eyes flitting around the paneled room. "Strange."

"What's strange, Mr. Budlong?" asked Nancy Spencer.

"This castle. Everything about this place." His eyes seemed unfocused, like those of one in a trance. "It's almost as though I am living something over again. I keep feeling that I have been here before. A long time ago."

"A sense of *déjà vue!*" Mrs. Spencer almost whispered.

Jim Spencer cast a startled glance at his wife. "Well, you *were* here before, Homer. Several times. Maybe that's what you remember."

"No, it's more than that, Jim. It's Auchterlony and the countryside. The whole thing. It's the scent of the bog myrtle—the way the light shatters against the hills beyond Glen Arley. It's all new to me, and yet, in a way I cannot understand, it's all familiar." He emitted a small laugh, almost of embarrassment. "When I left in the helicopter the day of the Games, I had the weirdest feeling that forces out of the past were trying to touch me. To hold me."

Jim Spencer looked uncomfortable. "Now, Homer, the only force that touched you that day was the caber that almost brained you! Maybe you were still feeling the effects of that when you climbed on board the chopper."

Homer Budlong grunted. "I suppose." He nodded as though convincing himself. "Yeah, that's the way it must have been." He shrugged. "Where were we, Jim?"

"We just reviewed the sales figures, Homer, and if they were any better it would merely be a disaster! As it is—" Jim Spencer flung up his hands in a gesture of despair.

Kenny took a deep breath. It was now or never. And he owed it to his father. "Look, Mr. Budlong," he burst out, "it wasn't Dad's fault. I mean about the foul-up in the new flavor. I was the one who did it. And now I'll tell you how it happened."

"Kenny!" Jim Spencer's voice was almost a hiss. "You're not going to bring up that idiotic ghost business—"

"Ghost?" Homer Budlong's brows shot up. "What ghost?"

"The one who lives upstairs," explained Kenny patiently.

"Oh, that one." Homer Budlong looked somewhat dazed.

"He's actually the ghost of the seventh Earl of Strathullen. He died in 1568."

"Hm," said Homer Budlong.

"He died right after Mary Queen of Scots arrived in the castle after escaping from prison. He was afraid to help her because he could have lost his head and all his lands. There was someone with the queen that night, a big strong fellow—I guess a guy a lot like you, Mr. Budlong—" Now, why had he said *that?*

"Like me?" Homer Budlong looked startled.

"Right, sir. Anyway, this big fellow was really mad at the earl and he laid this curse on him—"

"And that's why he's a ghost? Because this big guy cursed him?" It was hard to tell from the expression on Homer Budlong's face whether he was incredulous or merely amused.

Kenny nodded solemnly. "That's why his body can't rest in the little cemetery of St. Fillan. And why no grass can grow on top of the grave." He hesitated. "Maybe I ought not to tell you, Mr. Budlong, but he's awfully mad at you for moving all those toffee machines into his castle."

"His castle?" The Californian frowned. "Kenny, we *paid* for the castle!"

"I know, but—"

"It was in our last stockholders report." Mr. Budlong looked hurt.

"I don't think he's a stockholder, sir. Anyway, he misses the peace and the quiet he had before we got here. He'd like it if we all went away."

A small smile played around Homer Budlong's hard mouth. "Of course, Kenny, you understand

I'd have to explain all this to our directors back in California. I'm afraid they're a cynical lot. They don't believe in much, and I'm pretty sure that includes a Scottish ghost. Can you tell me a little more about him?"

"Well, he's real small with deep-set eyes, and his face is gray and kind of timid like. He wears a kilt and a Highland bonnet with a chief's feather. And his shoes have gilt buckles—"

"Buckles?" Budlong's face was suddenly alert, thoughtful. "That first day I got here somebody tripped me. Somebody with a buckle on his shoe—" His voice trailed off. "And the hand that touched me was small. Like a child's hand. Strange."

Jim Spencer, who had been listening in smoldering exasperation, darted a grim look at his son. "You bet it's strange, Homer! It's more than strange, it's nuts! After all, we're living in the twentieth century, even here in Auchterlony, and ghosts—"

"You say he wore a kilt, Kenny?" interposed Homer Budlong. "Could you describe it?"

"It's a tartan I'd never seen before, sir. Dark green and blue squares with thin white stripes."

Homer Budlong sucked in his breath. "That was the tartan the little guy was wearing when he clobbered me! Like the Graham tartan but with a little less green."

Jim Spencer looked at him curiously. "Didn't realize you knew so much about tartans, Homer."

"Oh, well." The big man laughed almost apologetically. "It's a bit of a hobby of mine. After food. Maybe I never told you this, Jim, but our family is Scottish. A way, way back. Came to California from Cape Breton Island in Canada."

"Come to think of it, Homer, I do remember your mentioning something about the old clansmen being your kind of guys. Funny, I never really connected it, though."

"Budlong?" Mrs. Spencer was frowning. "I'd never have guessed it as a Scottish name."

The visitor grinned. "It isn't. My father died when I was an infant. When my mother remarried, I was given the name of my stepfather." He chewed the loose tobacco from the end of his cigar. "Actually, I was born a MacSpurtle."

Kenny felt the blood freeze solid in his veins. "A what?" he finally managed.

"A MacSpurtle. Kind of an unusual name. Come to think of it, I've never run into anyone who had it."

Too stunned to talk, Kenny said nothing. As though isolated from the others, he was only dimly conscious of the voices around him. They seemed to come from far away, remote from his own private world. All he was aware of at the moment was the whirling confusion deep inside him. The little ghost had said that the MacSpurtles were a vanished clan. That none of that name existed. Yet Mr. Budlong had been born a MacSpurtle. And he was very much alive. . . . Kenny suddenly realized that his father was speaking, and that he was speaking with anger in his voice.

"It's all right, Homer, for you to come over here and chat about ghosts, but I have other things on my mind! Like that nasty cable you sent me relieving me of my responsibilities. Well, I did my best, but if that's the way you feel about it, then good riddance! I can always get another job."

Homer Budlong glowered. "Nasty cable! What's the matter with you, Jim? You *have* another job! That's why I had to take you off the Fraser assignment. Didn't that idiot Hepplewaithe mention that in the message? Well, my fault. I should have checked the cable."

Jim Spencer said dully, "I have a new job?"

"You sure have. You're coming over to Beverly Hills. You and Ian Cameron. Good man, that! Want Ian to help you run my new fast-food operation in California. We've already test-marketed it in the Santa Barbara area and it's a sensation! I'd like you and Ian to take the concept and run with it nationally." The president of UGH breathed hard, his eyes aglow with excitement. "We'll murder the competition! Nobody else has anything like it! We'll keep the formula a company secret, like Coca-Cola. We'll—"

"For heaven's sakes, Homer!" exploded Jim Spencer, unable to control his curiosity a moment longer. "What is it?"

"Eh? That's right, I didn't tell you." A sly grin creased his heavy face. "It's Mrs. Wheerie's Forfar Bridies."

"What?" exclaimed Jim Spencer.

"No!" gasped Nancy Spencer.

"*Our* Mrs. Wheerie?" ejaculated Kenny.

"*Our* Mrs. Wheerie," thundered Homer Budlong. He seemed to be enjoying himself. "I say that because she's now on the company's management payroll. She's coming over to Beverly Hills as Special Products Director until we get things rolling. I have ambitious plans for Mrs. Wheerie in California. She's got an instinct about foods. Like myself."

"Does she know?" asked Jim Spencer. "I mean, about coming over to California?"

Homer Budlong winked and nodded. "We had

to handle the whole thing hush-hush. Didn't want the competition to learn our little game. Sorry I couldn't tell you what was going on, Jim." He drew his hand across his jaw in a bemused way. "Funny thing, come to think of it, but Mrs. Wheerie didn't seem too surprised when I told her. It was almost as though she had known all the time what I was planning. But that's crazy."

"What about Fraser's?" It was Jim Spencer who asked the question.

"Oh, Fraser's?" Mr. Budlong frowned. "I think I'll make arrangements to get rid of it." For some reason, unusual in a man of such self-assurance, he looked uncomfortable. Almost embarrassed. "Somehow, I don't think it was the right take-over for us. The wrong chemistry, I guess. I understand there's a Dundee marmalade company that's interested in taking it off our hands. Maybe they can do a better job with it." He spoke a little too loudly. Too defiantly. He shuffled his papers as though anxious to get on to other matters.

Jim Spencer looked at him curiously. "Funny thing, Homer, I've never seen you run away from a challenge before."

The Californian's face got beet red. "I'm not running away from a challenge, Jim Spencer! I don't run away from anything or anybody! It's just that—" He seemed to be waiting for the words to come and, when they didn't, the indignation and resentment drained from his face. After a long moment he said quietly, "I'm going to tell you folks something. Something I've told no one before. I just hope it doesn't sound too melodramatic in the telling.

"Everybody who knows me is convinced I'm some sort of machine, a robot without feelings. Maybe it's my fault. Maybe it's an image I've cultivated. But it's only an image. And it's not me.

"What is it that's got me to where I am today? I'll tell you. It's something within me that guides me whenever I have to make a major decision. Computer print-outs are fine and Harvard Business grads can be a lot of help, but it's that small voice deep inside me that I listen for. And that small voice tells me now to sell Fraser's."

Jim Spencer frowned. "You said something earlier, Homer. Something I found—well—strange. It had to do with reliving certain events that might have happened long ago. Did any of this have any bearing on your decision?"

Homer Budlong hesitated. "Maybe. I'm not quite sure. I sense that it did. I just have this eerie sensation that I did something to someone once, perhaps in this very castle, that I now bitterly regret." He shook his head. "I know the whole thing sounds crazy, Jim. Still, I guess all Celts are mystics at heart."

"But, Homer!" exclaimed Jim Spencer. "All this talk about reliving the past! I mean, the idea of reincarnation . . ."

"I'm not talking about any ideas, Jim. I'm talking about the senses. About the things of the mind. And now that Kenny here has told me his story, I'm more convinced than ever that I should sell Fraser's and get out of Strathullen Castle."

"Will ye have another Forfar Bridie, Mr. Budlong?" It was Mrs. Wheerie who asked the question. She had changed since serving them lunch and was wearing a smart lavender-colored dress with touches of white. A little powder had banished both the creases and the pallor from her cheeks. There was a hint of a smile as she advanced toward the table, a platter in her hand.

"Thanks, Mrs. Wheerie, don't mind if I do." Homer Budlong waited until she had left the dining room before turning to Mr. and Mrs. Spencer. "Fascinating creature, that! Did you know she's buried four husbands? Hope her luck is a lot better in California."

"I'm sure it will be," murmured Mrs. Spencer. She looked thoughtfully toward the kitchen.

"So that was why you kept calling us to send you Forfar Bridies," Jim Spencer said. "You were test-marketing?"

Homer Budlong frowned. "You didn't think I was going to eat twelve dozen of them at a clip myself?" He looked hurt. "I mean, Jim, I love to eat, but there's a limit."

"Sorry, Homer. By the way, when do you want Ian and me over in California?"

"Just as soon as you both can get yourselves packed. Your families can follow at any time." He eased himself out of his chair and glanced at his watch. "Two o'clock already? I'll have to be moving." He snapped his briefcase shut. "Don't bother seeing me off, Jim. I've got a car waiting outside. Have to be in London before five. There's a Yorkshire pudding company down there that might have good vibes."

"Yorkshire pudding?" repeated Jim Spencer. "Good vibes?" He shrugged, then laughed. "Good luck, Homer."

"See you all in Beverly Hills!" Homer Budlong poked his head into the kitchen. "You too, Mrs. Wheerie!" The next moment he was across the room and gone.

"Well, how about that?" exclaimed Nancy Spencer. "Good-bye Auchterlony, hello Beverly Hills! At least you can't say that life at UGH is dull. And it's marvelous that the Camerons are coming!"

"*And* Mrs. Wheerie." There was a grin on Jim Spencer's face as he glanced toward the kitchen. "When you get to know her, she's really quite a gal. Still, I can't figure out what she expects to find in California."

Nancy Spencer gave him a level look. "Among other things, she expects to find a husband."

"What?" gasped Kenny's father. "Number Five?"

Mrs. Spencer moved an indolent shoulder. "You men. Didn't you notice her clothes? And the new look in her eyes? Mrs. Wheerie very definitely is back in circulation again."

"But who—?" began Jim Spencer.

"Someone with similar interests," interrupted his wife. "Or to put it another way, someone with an instinct for foods."

"Someone with an instinct for foods—" Jim Spencer's jaw dropped. He stared at his wife. "Nancy! You're not suggesting that husband Number Five is going to be—"

"Wait and see," purred Mrs. Spencer. "A woman has an instinct about these things. I'm not quite sure if *he* knows it yet, but Mrs. Wheerie does. I caught the look in her eyes as she studied him a little while ago. He's been a bachelor too long, and I guess she feels the same way about being a widow. It's an ideal setup. Plus the shared passion for food. See if I'm not right, Jim Spencer."

"You could be right, Nancy. And did you hear what Homer said? That Mrs. Wheerie didn't seem surprised about going to California? Maybe she had the whole thing planned right from the beginning."

"Which helps explain something else, Jim. Why

she was so positive there was no one living in the castle. She didn't want anything to happen that might discourage the Americans from staying." She suddenly laughed explosively. "Dear Mrs. Wheerie! I'm going to love being with her in California. How about you, Jim?"

Kenny did not wait to hear what his father might say. He was already racing upstairs to find Mr. MacDhu and tell him the sensational news.

That the Clan MacSpurtle was not extinct. And that Homer Budlong was a MacSpurtle!

🔆 *17*

"M r. MacDhu?" Kenny whispered as he peered around the room with the portrait over the mantelpiece. He waited, his heart throbbing, for an eagle feather to come drifting through the air. For a soft voice with an up-and-down lilt to it to break the oppressive silence. But no eagle feather materialized. No soft voice broke the stillness.

He hesitated, conscious of a wash of bitter disappointment deep within him. This was Mr. MacDhu's old room. The room in which he had said they could always meet. Yet, come to think of it, the little ghost had not been there the last time Kenny had looked for him. That had been right after the toffee machinery had been set up and Mr. MacDhu had gone into hiding. All at once Kenny caught his breath. Of course! Why had he not thought of it sooner! The old stone bench by the sundial! Certain in his heart he would find his friend lurking somewhere around the sunken garden, Kenny retreated quickly from the room.

His mind was a caldron of bubbling, seething thoughts as he hastened toward the east wing, his footsteps echoing eerily in the deserted gallery. *Had* Mr. Budlong been fantasizing when he spoke of having been here before, of reliving things that had happened long ago? What had been behind his recollection of an injustice he had done to someone in Strathullen Castle, an injustice he now bitterly regretted? And why, of all the names in the world, should he have been born with that of MacSpurtle? Had it been chance that brought him here? Coincidence? Or were there forces at work in this remote corner of the Scottish Highlands that defied rational explanation?

There were a lot of other things on Kenny's mind that he was eager to share with Mr. MacDhu. The startling news, for instance, that Mr. Budlong was giving up Fraser's Toffee and that Mr. MacDhu would once again have the castle all to himself. And of course the news about the transfer to California, and about Mrs. Wheerie going over there, too. As Special Products Director, no less! Oh, there would be much to talk about when he and Mr. MacDhu got together! Kenny found himself sprinting the last fifty yards, and his feet were fairly flying as he burst into the secluded grove at the end of the garden. He stopped dead in his tracks as his eyes took in the scene before him. There was the sundial. And there was the ancient stone bench. But there was no Mr. MacDhu.

"Are you there?" he called softly. "If you're hiding, there's nothing to be afraid of. Not any more. Mr. Budlong's gone and the toffee machines will be gone soon. The castle will be yours again, just as it always was. Mr. MacDhu—" He stopped, suddenly aware of how foolish he would look should someone chance by and find him talking to himself. He hesitated, took one final look around the deserted grove, then slowly made his way back to the castle.

The days that followed were days of bitter disappointment to the boy. Search how he might, there was no trace of the small ghost anywhere. Duggie insisted on helping too, and for one entire day the boys methodically went from room to room and scoured every foot of the extensive grounds without result. It was as though Mr. MacDhu had simply vanished into thin air, as well as he might have.

One afternoon three weeks later, when Kenny had finished helping his mother pack the trunks for the trip home, he suddenly realized that this might well be his last chance to visit Auchterlony and Glen Arley. A lot of things had happened since the day he had first seen them. For all he knew, it might be a long time before he came back this way again, if ever. He might as well start saying his good-byes now.

Black rags of cloud scudded across the sky and a drift of cold rain stung his face as he approached the fringes of Glen Arley. The wind, blowing across the empty reaches of the glen, carried a remembrance of hawthorn and warm summer grasses. Far off in the distance he spotted the great cairn of stones where Duggie and he had chatted. He let his eyes drift away from the cairn and on an impulse turned and stared back in the direction he had just come. The great bulk of Strathullen seemed even more awesome from afar than near. He squinted against the soft rain to

181

study the castle better. Somehow it was still hard to believe that it was to this very building that Mary Queen of Scots had fled on that fateful night so long ago.

The rain had stopped by the time he circled back around the village, and a coquettish sun was flirting from behind a fan of amber cloud. He wended his way along High Street, its round cobbles glistening from the rain that had just fallen. Letting his feet guide him, he found himself strolling along the narrow lane behind the red-bricked Fraser building. Lost in thought, he was startled a few moments later to find himself at the entrance to the ancient chapel of St. Fillan. He stared around him, confused and puzzled. What was he doing here? He had been daydreaming, of course, letting his mind wander off with his feet. Yet it seemed odd that he should have come here. Very odd.

The crumbling chapel was as he had last seen it, entangled in nettles and weeds, with stunted bracken protruding from clefts in the cracked stone. Great swaths of ivy encircled the few erect pillars, for all the world like sinuous green snakes, frozen in space. The empty windows still stared with dead eyes at the far-off emptiness of Glen Arley. And in the little cemetery, the sagging iron chains still marked the last resting-place of the mighty earls of Strathullen. The last resting place of all, that is, but one of them. The one who had been doomed by a frightful curse from ever knowing the peace of his clansmen.

Kenny hesitated by the gate. What was there to see inside the little kirkyard, anyway? He had been there before. A stricken plot of earth, barren of life, where no flowers grew and no grass flourished. Still, this was the last time he would be here. As long as he had come this far, he might as well take the opportunity to pay his final respects to his small friend.

The iron gate creaked open on its rusty hinges as he made his way to the grave of the seventh Earl of Strathullen. Everything was as it had been before. The rust-flecked chain around the plot. The tombstone, and the simple inscription—the faded lettering, the elegant curlicues partially obliterated by time and weather. The barren soil— He stopped, his breath a sudden heaviness in his lungs. No! It couldn't be true! But it was! There, thrusting through the bitter earth, like the tips of small, pointed lances, were myriads of fresh green shoots!

A sob of joy, of wonder, of unbelief broke from his lips as he fell to his knees alongside the grave.

Like one in a dream he extended his fingers and brushed them against the young grass blades, still wet from the rain. He stared, not quite comprehending what had happened. Knowing only that the barren soil was no longer barren. That where there had been death there was now life.

And all at once he knew with a terrible certainty that the awful curse of Calum MacSpurtle had been lifted. And that after four hundred years the soul of the seventh Earl of Strathullen was at peace with his ancestors. It was no wonder he had been unable to find the little ghost at home. He had already gone home.

How had it all happened? Perhaps he would

never really know. Mr. MacDhu had certainly been around the day Kenny chose the wrong toffee flavor, but there had been no hint at all of his presence since Mr. Budlong revealed he was a MacSpurtle. Only a MacSpurtle could lift the curse. What were the words he said that day? *"I just have this eerie sensation that I did something to someone once, perhaps in this very castle, that I now bitterly regret."*

Yet that didn't make sense. How could Mr. Budlong have remembered something that took place over four hundred years ago? Kenny scowled. It would be awfully hard to explain that to anybody. Still, come to think of it, it would be just as hard to explain Mr. MacDhu to anyone. Unless of course a person believed in ghosts and the things that are not of this world.

High above the deserted churchyard of St. Fillan a curlew drifted on gently vibrating wings, its melancholy cry trailing behind it. Kenny watched it until it vanished beyond Glen Arley. Then he turned and made his way back to Strathullen Castle.

About the Author

WILLIAM MACKELLAR, who was born in Glasgow, Scotland, came to the United States at the age of eleven. He was educated in New York area schools and lived for many years on Long Island.

During World War II, he served for four years in the Signal Corps, three of them in North Africa, France, and Italy. A furlough in Scotland gave him the chance to revisit childhood scenes and to reawaken his interest in the Scottish countryside, which has since served as background for many of his stories. Later he spent four years in Europe as advertising manager of a large American corporation.

In addition to his Scottish stories, Mr. MacKellar has written dog, sports, and mystery stories, as well as short stories and light verse. Some of his more popular titles are *Wee Joseph, The Witch of Glen Gowrie, Alfie and Me and the Ghost of Peter Stuyvesant,* and *The Silent Bells.*

The author now lives in West Hartford, Connecticut, with his wife, two sons, a daughter, a perky West Highland terrier named Bonnie, and a cat named Alfie.

About the Artist

W. T. MARS was born in Poland and is a graduate of the Academy of Fine Arts in Warsaw. He painted and exhibited in Poland, and served for five years in the Polish Army in World War II. Later he worked in England and executed murals for the Festival of Britain. After having lived in Scotland for three years, he moved to the United States, where he now resides in Forest Hills, New York. Mr. Mars has illustrated over 250 books, mostly for young readers.

F
MAC

MacKellar, William

Kenny and the
Highland ghost

© THE BAKER & TAYLOR CO.